SEEKING HOPE

The Emergence Saga - Book One

Kim Cresswell

KC Publishing

For Justin, Carla, Porter, Peyton, and Leo

In memory of Mary Beech

Death leaves a heartache no one can heal,
love leaves a memory no one can steal.
— From a headstone in Ireland

ABOUT THE AUTHOR

Kim Cresswell resides in Ontario, Canada, and is the award-winning author of the action-packed Whitney Steel romantic suspense series. As a multi-genre author, her books have been featured online at *USA Today*, *NBC*, *FOX*, *Publishers Weekly*, *Booklife*, and *Scifi-Pulse.net*. The Assassin Chronicles TV series was in development with Council Tree Productions. The TV series is based on Kim's paranormal thriller novel, *Deadly Shadow*, and the highly anticipated sequel, *Invisible Truth*.

Want to learn more about the author? Sign up for Kim's newsletter. Join Kim Online:

www.kimcresswell.ca
Bookbub
Facebook
Twitter
Instagram

ABOUT SEEKING HOPE

A near extinction-level event. A dead world with new rules where freedom comes with a price.

Five years after a bioweapon called the XBU Virus is accidentally released from a Canadian government laboratory and eradicates 99.5 percent of the global population, survivors Astra Fallon and her best friend Jude Waverly emerge from her family's underground bunker in the rural municipality of Springfield, Manitoba, with nothing more than the will to survive. With food dwindling, they set out to find Astra's younger sister, Hope, who had been taken at the beginning of the outbreak to a government compound known as The Closure because of her possible rare immunity to the supervirus. But Astra and Jude quickly discover the compound is no longer a government-secured scientific sanctuary when they come face to face with Ayden Webb's end-of-the-world religious cult and Astra is forced to make a sacrifice she never imagined.

*There are two problems for our species'
survival - nuclear war and environmental
catastrophe - and we're hurtling towards
them. Knowingly. — Noam Chomsky*

CHAPTER ONE

Springfield, Manitoba - 2028

Day 1,825

It's strange what goes through your mind when you know freedom is on the other side of the door, but there could be a lot of other things—very bad things. Astra Fallon had no idea which way this was going to go. At the bottom of the stairs of her family's concealed underground bunker, she glanced at her best friend, Jude. A tight knot formed in her stomach. "Are you ready for this?"

His blue eyes met hers, the worry obvious by his furrowed brow. "I think so. We'll be out of food by the end of the day." He handed her a pair of sunglasses then put on a pair of stylish silver-framed aviators, knowing the drastic difference in the light would take time for their eyes to adjust.

Living underground for five years without sunlight

and fresh air had been tough, more for her, than Jude. He took it in stride, as he did with most things. His laid-back personality was one of the reasons they became friends in the first place. Not Astra. She was anxious and couldn't wait to feel the sun against her skin and inhale outside air instead of the bunker's temperature-controlled air circulating through the advanced military-grade filtration system. After putting on her sunglasses, she exhaled a nervous breath and waited for him to get one of her father's guns, in case they ran into any problems.

When the news that a deadly virus had been accidentally released from a Canadian lab, it was like any other Friday morning. She and Jude were seniors, attending first-period math class at South Fork High School, passing notes back and forth, making plans for the weekend with their friends. Principal Garver's panicked voice suddenly came over the PA system. He ordered everyone to return home immediately, shelter in place, that a deadly virus had been leaked, and it was highly transmissible, more contagious than anything ever seen before.

At first, people thought it was a joke, a conspiracy much like the Covid-19 pandemic eight years before. By the next day, widespread panic had broken out and with it came radical solutions including the hoarding of fuel, food, and supplies. Borders closed. Within two weeks, martial law came into effect pretty much worldwide and people fought back citing it was infringing on their rights. There was much talk and suspicions that the virus had been deliberately released through a secret government program to deal with overpopulation. The conspiracy theorists were wrong.

Entire cities were gutted by fires set by looters and those who refused to accept the truth. By the end of the first year, lawlessness broke out, even more, leaving destruction, paranoia, and despair as thousands of dead bodies filled the streets. The second year brought global protests and riots that ended up infecting most of the remaining survivors who hadn't followed the strict protocols issued at the beginning to keep them alive. Supply chains were wiped out. Food became scarce with no one to plant or harvest the crops or feed and care for the farm animals. Food production plants sat idle. Governments collapsed along with the economy leaving countries in ruins, unable to contain the supervirus or the deadly chaos. By the fourth year, the world went silent. It was then when Astra realized no one was going to save them. They were on their own.

Her parents had told her the virus was wicked and smart by design, a bioweapon the government had been testing, following three dangerous months of escalating nuclear tensions with North Korea. No one wanted a nuclear holocaust and that's where the world was heading if North Korea couldn't be stopped. The XBU Virus was the solution according to governments around the world. Take out the country's population and rid the world of the nuclear threat. Instead, the virus with a one-hundred-percent fatality rate had been unintentionally released and had killed almost everyone.

The hybrid chimera pathogen wasn't a typical virus. It was made up of genes from two other viruses and a new genetically engineered toxin to create a lethal viral load. The virulent contagion was merciless, spread by respiratory droplets and aerosols. When infected, the vector destroyed the blood vessels, disintegrating them into mush. Tissue death followed and then septic shock. Death happened rapidly, within twenty-four hours. At least no one had suffered for weeks or months.

From what she had heard on the news, on various social media accounts, and videos streaming on the Internet, thousands of children across the country had been rounded up, whisked away from grade schools, and tested to see if they were immune in hopes of creating a viable vaccine. Her sister, Hope, was one of the children. Unfortunately, it was too late to get enough of the new mRNA-V2 vaccine out quickly enough to stop the spread. Most of the world's population had already died.

Astra wasn't sure if Hope was still alive. She needed to know. Her sister had to be terrified after being ripped from her family and taken away by strangers.

Not once had Astra thought about giving up. If they were going to risk going out to search for food, they would find Hope and bring her home, a promise she had made to her father. She always kept her promises and this one was more important than ever.

Being confined underground had been brutal, a bleak existence, their life consisting of four steel walls. She missed her friends, family, attending high school, and working part-time. Astra worried every day about the animals that had been under her care at the local rescue. She hoped her coworkers had released them from their cages before the workers died from the virus. Her gaze strayed to the open-plan bunker with two bedrooms, a large bathroom, spacious kitchen, a cold storage room, camera surveillance, and LED windows that simulated outdoor nature scenes controlled by remote control. She rubbed her temples. The ceiling's bright lights had given her a headache again or maybe it was the anticipation of finally walking out the door after five years. Astra wasn't sure which.

Jude pocketed a handful of shotgun shells. "Are you scared?"

A shiver ran through Astra, and she lied. "Not really." She was terrified of what they would discover on the outside. "Are you?"

He hesitated for a second and had an unreadable expression on his face. "Maybe a bit."

Astra looked up the stairs again at the gas-tight steel door with an electronic keypad and lock. No matter what they were about to walk into, good or bad, their future was about to begin, whether they were ready or not.

CHAPTER TWO

T he glorious warmth of the sun touched the side of Astra's face and her skin crawled at the revolting pungent odor coming from the west. "The air reeks of death."

Jude's pale skin gleamed in the blinding sunlight, and he frowned. "It smells like rotting corpses. Man, that stinks."

A wave of nausea rolled through her, and the words froze on her lips. "Do you think the stench will ever go away?"

It had been a gamble going above ground. They both knew it. Neither of them was prepared for the reality. Death was all around them. Billions had died around the world. There was no escaping the rancidness in the May late-morning breeze. Jude had her father's favorite Remington 870 shotgun resting on his shoulder. Luckily, they both knew their way around guns, thanks to their fathers who had hunted like many of the residents in the rural area.

He shrugged. "Maybe."

His dark brown hair was much longer, in need of another trim. He was over six feet tall, square-shouldered, strong in a sport's jock kind of way. He looked handsome in a white t-shirt and jeans, older, more mature in the natural light.

They had been seventeen when the plague had begun. Confined like prisoners in the thirty by sixty-foot underground bunker on her family's ten-acre property with no outside human contact, the loneliness would have driven her insane if Jude hadn't been with her.

"Are you sure your parents said the virus would probably burn itself out after it killed most of its hosts?" Jude asked.

Astra's chest squeezed and she gulped down the hard lump in her throat. Tears formed at the corners of her eyes.

Her parents were two of four leading epidemiologists with the National Microbiology Laboratory in Winnipeg, the country's only CL4 virology laboratory where the bioweapon had been released. The lab was one of only a few in the world equipped to work with Risk Group 4 pathogens, the highest biohazard classification. The CDC had categorized the XBU virus as a 'Category A' bioterrorism agent and described the toxin as the deadliest pathogen to humans ever seen. Images flashed in the back her mind. She could still hear her parent's voices in her head as if they were standing in front of her.

"Astra, you know what to do. We've discussed it many times," her father said, gasping for a breath. "Don't leave the bunker for five years. Everything you need is there. If anyone finds the hidden entrance, don't let them in no matter how much they beg. And keep Jude with you at all times."

There was a long pause of silence before she heard her father's voice again. "We spoke with Jude's parents...they're infected too."

Astra's stomach sank.

"You need to understand what this means," her mother said, sobbing. "We aren't going to make it—we're going to die. It's up to you and Jude now. I love you."

At first, Astra struggled to decipher what her mother's words meant. "Mom, I love you." Tears streamed down her cheeks. "Please, I can't do this. Daddy, I'm scared."

"Hunny, I know you are. You're young, smart, and resilient. You and Jude will get through this together. We know you will. You're in good hands."

She heard her mother crying in the background and then she went into a horrifying long coughing fit. The reality of the situation took hold of Astra, and she couldn't think straight. This can't be happening. Her parents...Jude's...everyone was dying. She wiped the tears from her face with the back of her hand and heard her father's choked voice.

"Go to The Closure. It's safe there. Find Hope and bring her home. Promise you'll find her."

Grief tore at Astra's insides, and she blew out a shaky breath. "Daddy...I promise."

Astra's entire world crumbled in an instant. She had cried for days until she couldn't cry anymore. Jude had cried too after his phone call with his parents. He didn't think she'd noticed. He still had a defined sadness in his voice. They both did.

"Hey? Are you okay?" Jude's voice sliced through the crippling thoughts.

She shook the god-awful memories away. "I'm fine. That's what they told me. We should still be careful if we come into contact with anyone just in case. We still have lots of masks, gloves, and disinfectant."

"That's about all we've got left."

Concern bubbled up inside her and her stomach rumbled. Astra was hungry and sick of being hungry. She missed her mother's cooking and the Sunday family dinners. She'd give anything for a real meal, not the MREs they'd been living on, or the millionth can of baked beans and canned tuna. They had rationed every morsel of food, spent every day staying busy by reading, playing board games, exercising, binge-watching DVDs, and watching TV until every station on the air turned to crackling static.

Behind her, leaves rustled in the dense under-growth. Astra turned her head and followed the noise. She tried to convince herself the sound was nothing, that she had imagined it.

Jude spun and aimed the shotgun at the line of trees along the road.

The rustling noise intensified. Branches swished and snapped. Something's out there. Her pulse sped up. "What do you think it is?" She craned her neck and searched the area for movement but didn't see any.

He grasped her arm and guided her behind him. "I don't know. Could be anything."

A spark of alarm lit in her chest. Or anyone. A survivor. They could be infected.

Suddenly, a thin German Shepard emerged from behind two Jack Pine trees. He zig-zagged toward them with his nose to the ground. Astra's pulse calmed and she let out a loud breath. "He looks hungry."

Jude kept the weapon pointed at the canine. "He might be mean."

The dog barked twice and approached, his body language, guarded. Astra crouched to the dog's level and waited for him to make contact. "It's okay, boy."

"Be careful. He could bite you." She tilted her head

and peered up at him. "Did you forget I worked at an animal shelter? He's fine. Just hungry and lost. I'm glad he found us."

Jude lowered the gun and grinned when the dog rubbed against her and nuzzled her neck. "I'll get him some water and a little to eat. We can't spare much. Then we need to check the house before we leave to see if we can find any food that hasn't gone bad."

As he walked past her, she looked up at him again. "Do you want to stop at your house and grab your things before we leave to find Hope?"

A muscle in his jaw twitched and he was silent for a long beat. "No."

Normally, her first instinct would be to ask him why. She already knew the answer. As heartbreaking as it was, at least her parents had died at work forty-five minutes away. As far as they knew, Jude's parents had succumbed to the virus at home, down the road from where they were standing. It was painful to think they were so close. He rarely spoke about his parents anymore and Astra wished she could read his mind. She cared about him deeply. Telling him how she felt would ruin their friendship. Despite his easy-going personality, he always shut down when it came to talking about feelings. Maybe one day he would be ready to talk.

When Jude returned with a big bowl of water and

a small handful of beef jerky, Astra continued to pet the dog as he gobbled down the meat. "What are we going to call him?"

Jude rubbed his chin and stared at the dog. "Raider. He's a great warrior."

The dog pricked his ears and tilted his head at him. Astra laughed. "I think he likes the name, even though he doesn't look much like a warrior right now."

"Hey, I don't want you to get too attached. Eventually, when there is nothing to eat, we might have to —"

Astra cringed. "Don't say that. You know how I feel about animals." She wrapped her arms around the dog's neck and hugged him. "We aren't going to do that ever. Promise me."

A beat of silence passed between them. "I promise." He patted the dog on the head. "Well, Raider, welcome to the end of the world. This is the best it gets. I guess you're coming with us."

* * *

While Jude finished loading their backpacks, food, water, and weapons into the back of Astra's father's double cab F-150 parked in the driveway, ominous dark cauliflower-shaped clouds swirled, blowing in from the east. Wind rattled the trees. The gale shoved against his back and sent dirt whirling around him.

He could taste the approaching storm on the tip of his tongue, the way the air pressure had changed. His shoulders tensed. He quickly stuffed a handful of garbage bags into the front pocket of his jeans and studied Astra in the driveway, running and playing with the dog. She looked more relaxed than usual and happier. Gravel crunched under her feet as her long auburn hair blew wildly in the wind. Dressed in jean shorts and a green tank-top, her clothes hung loosely on her body.

She had lost more weight, looked too skinny for her five-foot-seven frame. It wasn't difficult to lose weight when you had been rationing food for years. Since being confined, they had grown closer. He hadn't dared to tell her that he loved her, in fear of being rejected. It was probably better to remain friends anyway since they didn't know how long they would be able to survive this new world. Astra ran up to him, out of breath. Raider stuck to her like glue, and never left her side.

"Did the truck start okay?"

Jude nodded. "Took a couple of tries then it fired right up. I always thought it was strange that your father kept the truck hidden in the woods behind the house. Makes perfect sense now."

"Dad was thinking about the future, the next big pandemic, and how we would survive." A faint smile crossed her lips. "He called it our 'emergency vehicle'.

If looters had found it, they would have stripped it clean."

"Especially, the high-wattage solar trickle charger on the dash to charge the battery. Your father was a very smart man."

After putting on their N95 respirator masks, Jude slung the shotgun over his shoulder, and they walked up the driveway toward the front steps of the house. The outside of the white-trimmed ranch-style home looked the same as it had five years before except some of the windows were grimy and cracked. Other windows were smashed, completely gone. The front yard was overgrown with towering weeds. He'd never seen grass and weeds so tall before. Trash and clothing were scattered across the lawn. The property and road were eerie quiet. No planes. No traffic. No farmers in the fields. Astra stopped at the bottom of the stairs and pointed at the partially open front door.

Jude knew the unsecured house would have been easy pickings for strangers. The breeze picked up and tore through the trees causing the door to swung back and forth in a western-saloon kind of way. He had watched enough western movies over the past five years since Astra's father had been a western movie fanatic and kept most of his DVDs in the bunker.

Cautiously, taking one step at a time, his gut twisted

in knots. He'd learned to always trust his gut instinct. It was rarely wrong. Everything told him to turn around and leave but they needed to find some food. On the porch, he sucked in a slow breath and raised the shotgun to chest level prepared to shoot anyone who might be inside. This was about survival. Theirs. He had never shot or killed anyone. The thought of hurting anyone made him uneasy. Things were different know. He would do whatever he had to do to protect Astra. With his parents and friends gone, she was all he had left.

Darker clouds swiftly moved in and swallowed what was left of the blue sky. Low-pitched thunder rumbled in the distance. Raider trotted past them without a care in the world, up the stairs, and into the house. With the shotgun still raised, Jude shoved the door open with the toe of his boot and waited a few seconds before entering. Adrenaline surged.

Astra glanced at him and spoke in a hushed voice. "Be careful."

Inside, a ghastly strong smell hit him first. It smelled like a combination of sweet cheese, mold, feces, dirt, and rotten cabbage. Then flies.

Astra's hazel eyes went big and round. She gasped. "Look what they've done to the house!"

Adrenaline quickly dissipated. Unable to take his eyes off the scene, Jude lowered the gun and stared, astounded by the destruction. The once stylish great room featuring a stone fireplace, soaring oak ceilings, and two modern plush sofas had been completely ransacked. The white painted walls had been defaced with graffiti, spray-painted with brightly colored images, symbols, and names of people. Most of the furniture was broken and the picture frames containing Astra's family photographs were smashed to smithereens. The sofa cushions were slashed and covered in a thick layer of dirt and dust. Trash was strewn everywhere. Next to one of the sofas, four fly-infested corpses lay on the floor in various positions and stages of decomposition. Squatters, he figured. Jude felt his skin prickle with fear. Roadkill was the only way to describe what he was looking at. Normally, he had a stomach like steel, and nothing grossed him out, until now. Gut-churning nausea overwhelmed him. He inhaled and exhaled deep breaths to stop from throwing up.

The dog trotted out of one of the three bedrooms at the back of the house and pranced proudly past them with a long bone dangling from his mouth. He hightailed it out the front door.

Astra's face turned a shade of green. "Is that what I think it is?"

Jude's focus waned and he felt the blood drain from his face. "Looks like a shinbone and foot." She turned away and gagged. He thought for sure she was going to be sick inside her mask. Amazingly, she kept it together and so did he. If this was what her house looked like, he could only guess this would be the new normal everywhere. This wasn't the world he remembered. Not even close.

Nervousness formed in his gut, and he forced himself to concentrate. "We'll go room-to-room together. Stay clear of the bodies. Grab any food, supplies, clothing. Any food that's three months past the expiry date should still be safe to eat but I doubt anything is left."

Her eyes held a certain sadness. He could tell it was rough being home knowing her parents had died from the virus and seeing what desperate survivors had done to her home.

A dozen flies buzzed around her head. She swatted them away. "Some of my father's clothes might fit you."

"Whatever you think will work." Jude pulled out the garbage bags from his pocket and handed her a couple. "We should hurry. There's a nasty storm moving in."

Astra sighed. "Just what we need, bad weather." She took the bags and the same sadness resurfaced and reflected the back of her eyes.

He wanted to reassure her that everything would be okay, more out of hope than anything. Jude knew he couldn't. They were stuck in a waking nightmare and the odds were against them.

CHAPTER THREE

Speeding down the highway, heading west, prairie grass waved and flattened in the strong wind. Dirt and garbage rolled across the road like tumbleweed as horses and cows mulled about in the fields. It was strange, serene, not seeing any traffic on the road. While Jude drove, Astra clutched the last remaining photograph of her parents and Hope in her lap. Anger lodged inside her. All her family's keepsakes had been destroyed or were missing including her great grandmother's jewelry. The food situation had not been much better. All they found was a can of baked beans and a sleeve of unopened soda biscuits hidden in one of the bedroom closets. It was better than nothing. The refrigerator in the kitchen and the chest freezer in the basement that had always been packed full of meat was empty. Tightness gripped her chest. She couldn't make sense of what she'd witnessed in the house and couldn't shake the gruesome images of the rotting bodies. It was one thing to watch tragic events unfold on TV or online. It was another, to witness the grim aftermath in full technicolor and smell it.

Astra had a hard time visualizing in her mind what Winnipeg would look like with a population of almost a million. Fear thrummed through her, and she reminded herself that finding her sister was all that mattered. She shifted in the seat and glanced over her shoulder at Raider in the back seat with his muzzle stuck out the partly open window. His cheeks ballooned and his tongue wagged in the gushes of air. Thank goodness that he had buried his prize bone in the front yard before they'd left. He seemed loyal and probably had gone through a lot. It was as if he'd been with them all along. Astra smiled to herself. Having a dog made the terrible situation they were in a bit more bearable.

Leaning her head back on the headrest, fat rain-drops splattered against the windshield. Jude flicked the wipers on and hit the button to roll up the windows. Astra spotted countless abandoned cars, trucks, delivery, and transport trucks with damaged windows littering the shoulder and the inner lane of the highway. From what she could see, the vehicles were empty. She shivered at the memories during the first year of the outbreak, wishing she could erase them forever. She could still hear the fran-tic shrieks of shock and terror in her head coming from the angry mobs demanding answers and med-ical care. Astra understood their anger. Everyone was scared. Hospitals were overrun, taken over by terrified people with masked faces, their eyes wide with panic and fear. Massive makeshift tent cities popped up all over the world overcrowded with the hungry, infected, and dying. Astra never imagined she'd be stuck in the middle of a disaster like this. Not even in her worst nightmares.

Jude kept one hand on the steering wheel and tossed his sunglasses on the dashboard. She noticed the dark circles shadowing his eyes. Neither of them had slept well in anticipation of their 'freedom day' after being imprisoned underground below her family's home for what felt like an eternity.

"We have less than an eighth of a tank of fuel and the weather's getting worse," Jude said.

Astra frowned. "I doubt any of the stations have any fuel left. We'll have to swap the truck for a different vehicle." Considering how prepared her father had always been for any catastrophe, he habitually had forgotten to keep the truck filled with biodiesel. With global warming close to critical levels, governments united around the world had voted to replace gasoline in 2025 with environment friendly E92 biofuels, biodiesel made from vegetable oils and animal fats, as well as electric fuel cells that produced far less sulfur oxide, ozone, and carbon monoxide to help reduce the carbon footprint. Over ninety percent of the vehicles on the road before the virus outbreak were either electric or ran on biodiesel. The thought of her father made her sad. She missed her parents so much. Astra wondered if the ache in her heart would ever go away.

She stared out the side view window, longing for her old life, the ways thing used to be. Jude had received an acceptance letter to the College of Pharmacy, and she had been accepted into the University of Manitoba's pre-veterinary medicine program. He always wanted to be a pharmacist like his father and was eventually going to take over the family's drug store in Winnipeg. Their future had been ripped away in an instant. What did the future hold for them now? It was hard to believe they had one.

"You're probably right. The fuel pumps are likely be dry." The tense expression on his face melted away and he grinned. "Miss Astra, you get to choose our next vehicle."

She smiled. His voice was suave, her mother always said. In Astra's opinion, everything about Jude was charming even in the worst of times. "Any vehicle?"

"Yep. Whatever you want, if it runs on biodiesel. The world is your oyster. I know the world isn't much anymore, but we have to make the best of it." His white teeth flashed again. "We can speed, travel anywhere, do whatever we want. It's not as if anyone can stop us.

Astra knew he was only trying to lighten the mood.

His enthusiasm had always been infectious. She loved how he was so positive in the most difficult of times but worried he was compartmentalizing, dismissing the reality of their dire situation. Their life had changed in a heartbeat. They were two of very few survivors left on the entire planet. Astra wasn't sure if that had truly sunk in yet, for either of them. Her stomach grumbled reminding her how much they needed to find some more food. The last time she'd checked they had two small packages of beef jerky, one protein bar, a half bag of walnuts, a can of beans, crackers, and one MRE.

As they drove past the century-old cemetery where most of her relatives had been buried, the road twisted in a tight curve. A wall of rain hit the windshield like a giant wave and made it difficult to see. Her heart rate accelerated.

Jude gripped the wheel tighter until his knuckles turned white. He turned on the headlights and slowed the truck. His expression grew serious. "The pressure has dropped a lot more. The sky doesn't look right."

She peered in the side mirror at the dark sky with a weird hue of green behind them. Thunder boomed. Lightning flashed and seared the sky. Golf ball-sized hail bounced off the truck's windows like rubber balls and pummeled the roof. Her mouth went dry. "We'd better take cover."

"We'll be safer out of the truck. It isn't safe under the underpass." He stomped the gas pedal and the engine whined. Dirt, branches, and grass smacked hard against the windshield.

Raider barked and pawed at her arm, his overgrown nails biting into Astra's skin. She glimpsed over her shoulder at the dog, hoping to comfort him. Through the back window, her worst fear materialized. "Jude, floor it!"

* * *

Jude's eyes darted to the rear-view mirror at the monstrous funnel cloud in the distance sucking up dirt, vehicles, houses, and trees, then spitting them out in uncontrolled chaos. His heart wedged in his throat. There was no time to think. He gunned the engine and cranked the steering wheel to the left into the other lane. In a race against nature, he hotfooted down the highway trying to outrun the tornado. The fuel light dinged and blinked its last warning reminding him more trouble was on the way. Minutes later, he slammed on the brakes. The truck fishtailed to a stop at a forty-five-degree angle in the middle of the road. "Get in the ditch!" The truck shook violently, its headlights beaming, bouncing, slicing through the air.

Astra scrambled to release her seatbelt. She grabbed the door handle and couldn't open the door. Shoving it open with her feet, air blasted inside and made a high-pitched whistling sound throughout the cab. "The dog, the supplies. We can't leave them."

Terror strained her words and Jude tried to remain calm even though he was shaking. They couldn't leave behind the little they had. "I'll get everything. Get as low as you can in the ditch. Hurry!" Across the road, hydro poles split into two. Blue and orange sparks flashed. Electrical wires whipped and slashed through the air. His mind whirled as he watched Astra head in the opposite direction. The wind slammed her to her knees. His chest tightened and his heart drummed in his chest. "Get up!"

Astra finally got to her feet and stumbled forward taking awkward, unsteady steps then lurched through the vortex of air. She disappeared out of his view in the direction of the ditch.

Jude frantically jumped out of the truck. He pried open the back door with both hands as rain blasted sideways and slashed at this body. The dog jumped off the seat and into his arms. Jude ran. Fear boosted his speed and commitment to make it to safety. Soaking wet, he laid the dog in the deep trench next to Astra. Raider curled up against her, shaking.

Astra grabbed his wrist. "There's no time..."

Her voice disintegrated into the wind, and he couldn't make out what she was saying. He shook free and took a few steps. A burst of violent air caught his legs, and he went down face-first. Tangy warm blood filled his mouth. With a curse, Jude gritted his teeth and climbed to his feet. With his chest heaving, he snatched their backpacks and as many weapons as he could carry from the back of the truck. With a heavy backpack looped over each shoulder to help balance the weight, he sprinted back toward the ditch.

Astra frantically waved her arms, motioning behind him. He stumbled to a stop and glanced over his shoulder.

The truck spun like a top then slid sideways on two wheels down the road away from him and slammed into a car under the concrete underpass. Running faster, Jude threw the backpacks and supplies into the ditch. Then he dove in. Re-orienting himself, he crawled through the muddy water on his hands and knees. He caught Astra's hand. Dragging his battered body on top of hers and the dog's, he closed his eyes and covered his head with his arms, knowing the flying debris could easily seriously injure or kill them. Rapid breaths of air pulsed in and out of his lungs. He stayed flat, as still as possible, waiting it out, his heart pounding.

Complete blackness enclosed in around them. The wind roared and sounded like a freight train. Debris pelted his back, arms, and legs, lashing and piercing his skin. A sharp pain erupted in his back. Unaware of the extent of his injuries, Jude kept the side of his head pressed against hers and heard the dog whimpering and Astra crying.

Minutes passed and felt like hours. Then the world quieted.

As quickly as it began, the turbulent air dissolved into a light breeze, and the rain stopped. Patchy green-blue sky and thick marshmallow-looking clouds had replaced the darkness. It was as if nothing had happened. The tightness released in his chest. He rolled off Astra onto his back and sunk into three or four inches of water. His back throbbed with pain.

"Are you okay?" Astra asked.

He opened his eyes, his heart still racing. "Are you?"

"I've never been so scared in my life." Astra expelled a sharp breath, and her voice grew louder, angrier. "Don't ever do that again. You could have been killed."

His gaze traveled to Raider sitting on the side of the road above them, looking down at him. He understood why Astra was mad. He'd risked his life for the supplies. He had to. Jude had never seen her like this before. It was obvious she cared about him more than he had been aware of. He wasn't sure how to process the information since he felt the same about her. He grinned weakly and felt bad he had scared her. "I won't ever do it again. Promise."

Astra sat up covered with mud, her hair a tangled wet mess. Her eyes widened. "Jude, you're bleeding."

CHAPTER FOUR

"**I**'ll get the first aid kit." Stumbling through the ditch, Astra slipped and almost fell a couple of times. Mud sloshed inside her running shoes and between her toes. After locating their backpacks, she opened the black one, reached in, and found the plastic container with the first aid supplies. With her other hand, she pulled out two bottles of water from the bottom of the bag. Racing back, she found Jude sitting up with his head lowered. His bottom lip was split. Blood ran down his chin. Cuts, scrapes, and bruises scarred his arms and looked painful. Taking a seat next to him, she placed the first aid kit between her legs and lay the bottles of water beside her. "Do you hurt anywhere else besides your arms and lip?"

"Can you check my back? I swear something stabbed me."

A shiver of apprehension slid up her spine. Astra inched up the side of the ditch on her butt, enough to get behind him. Her jaw dropped open and her mind struggled to process what she was seeing. The back of his t-shirt was shredded as if a wild animal had attacked him. Astra gasped in horror when she saw the piece of wood was sticking out of his back just below his left lung. It appeared to be the length and width of a steak knife or a little bigger. It didn't look as if it was in very deep, but Astra wasn't sure. "You've got a piece of wood sticking in you."

Jude grunted. "Just pull it out."

A spark of concern edged his voice and made her more nervous. At first, she didn't want to touch the wood afraid she would hurt him. But he couldn't walk around like this. Astra drew a deep breath. She had to do this. Infection could set in. He could die. "You're probably going to need stitches and antibiotics."

"Just yank it out and bandage it up. Please, it hurts like hell. We don't have a suture kit." He licked his bloody lips. "My father always keeps extra antibiotics in the safe at the pharmacy for emergencies. I think this might be one of those times. We're only ten minutes away. We just have to get there."

Astra pulled the first aid kit to her and a bottle of water. She quickly rinsed the mud from her hands with some of the water then used what was left in the travel-sized bottle of hand sanitizer from the first aid kit. Astra pulled out a thick stack of gaze and a roll of medical tape. Wrapping her palm thick with gauze so she wouldn't end up with slivers, her fingers trembled. Placing her other hand flat against his back, she said, "Ready—One—two—three." Astra cringed and pulled out the piece of wood.

Jude jerked his head up. "Jesus, that hurt."

"I'm sorry." Dark crimson blood oozed and ran down his back. She quickly pressed a wad of gauze over the wound while he tore off pieces of tape with his teeth. When she was done taping the gauze in place, she inspected the rest of his back. Dozens of scratches and small cuts marked his back like his arms. Astra was grateful none of the other wounds appeared to be serious. "Here, take these." she handed him the last two aspirins from the first aid kit. He chewed the pills and downed the rest of the bottle of water in one big gulp.

After helping him to his feet, they climbed up the ditch and found the dog still sitting in the same spot, his tail wagging. She opened the other bottle of water, took a long drink, then tilted the bottle enough for the dog to lap up the rest.

Piles of broken branches and leaves covered areas on both sides of the road. A cow and two chickens lay dead a few feet away. Raider circled the lifeless bodies, sniffed them, then backed away. Astra grimaced. The poor animals never had a chance. Further ahead, a tree had been yanked out of the ground by its roots and laid across the other lane of the highway. Her gaze traveled to her father's scratched and dented pickup truck jammed up next to a small car.

Jude went and opened the driver-side door of the truck. He turned the ignition. The engine fired up then he shut it off. "Considering what it went through, it doesn't look too bad."

Astra glanced up at him, squinting in the sun. "What about fuel?"

He reached into the front pocket of his jeans and pulled out a switchblade he had found in the toolbox in the garage. "I'll check the car to see if it runs on biodiesel. If it does, I can cut a hose and siphon it out the fuel. If not, we'll have to walk it until we find another vehicle. Can you look around for something to put some fuel in, just in case? Don't wander too far."

She nodded and glanced at Raider. "Come on, boy. Let's see what we can find."

Five minutes later, grasping a gallon plastic milk jug she'd found inside a garbage bag tossed in the ditch on the other side of the underpass, Astra headed back to the truck. Raider stayed within a few feet of her, sniffing and peeing on everything he could. She stopped in her tracks when she saw Jude changing out of his wet clothes next to the truck with his back to her. The breath caught in his throat. In all the time they had spent together in the bunker, she hadn't seen him naked. Emotions knotted through her and part of her felt guilty for watching him. They were friends, had been friends throughout elementary and high school. Astra could not help but notice his well-defined muscular legs, butt, and shoulders. Something stirred inside her. He put on a pair of black pants and then carefully slid a baggie khaki-colored t-shirt over his head.

Not wanting to get caught watching him, she held the jug up in the air. "I found something."

He turned and his eyebrows raised. "That'll work." He took the container and gestured at the truck. "There're some clean clothes inside. I found a package of baby wipes in the glovebox of the car. You might be able to wash some of that mud off." He grinned. "You look like a swamp monster."

Astra peered down at her arms and legs covered in mud then back at him. "As if you looked any better before you changed." They both laughed.

While Jude was busy cutting a section of hose from the car's engine to use as a siphon, behind the truck Astra kicked off her shoes. Once she had cleaned herself with the wipes the best she could, she changed into a navy tank-top and black shorts. Glancing down at her soggy running shoes she leaned against the truck. They would have to do. It wasn't as if they had packed extra shoes. Astra bent down and pulled them on.

After getting their backpacks and supplies from the ditch loaded back into the truck, she climbed into the driver's seat. Weariness settled in her body. Jude laid down on the back seat and rested. Raider hopped onto the passenger seat, and she closed the door determined to get the antibiotics Jude needed before infection set in.

* * *

Ten minutes later, the sides of the road became less littered with vehicles. Astra slowed the truck and dread settled in the pit of her stomach like a concrete brick as she drove past the 'Pegasus welcomes you to The Peg' sign with the city's mascot, a white-winged horse from Greek mythology galloping in a night sky. She was haunted by the quietness, the stillness, and her family and friends that were gone. The city looked like what she envisioned Hell would look like minus the raging infernos. She felt as if she had entered some strange alternative universe. The air had an acrid smoky edge to it and reeked of sewage, corpses, and garbage. The sickening smell settled in her nostrils. Astra took in her surroundings, her gaze roaming the streets, shocked by the ravaged state of decay, dramatizing a new world, a brand-new fight.

Vehicles had been overturned and burned. Others that weren't burned-out shells still had human remains inside. She wanted to scream at the horrible devastation and human tragedy. Mangy dogs of all colors, breeds, and sizes wandered the street looking lost and hungry. She sighed audibly, barely able to hide her exasperation at their plight. A whirlwind of emotions brought tears to her eyes. Astra blinked them away determined to stay strong.

Four dogs sat in a row along the curb like the city's welcome committee. They barked and baring their fangs as if she was invading their turf, their town. Maybe she was. There was no human movement anywhere. Not a soul. Winnipeg was a ghost town. Dozens of feral cats scurried off the street and up onto the sidewalk when Astra drove by. In the parking lot next to her favorite pizza shop, a pack of twenty to thirty dogs gnawed on rotting bodies and bones piled high in mounds in what looked like at some point during the outbreak a tent morgue. Bile rose in her throat, and she swallowed it down. Two huge overflowing barrels of discarded masks and gloves guarded the entrance. The tent's faded green canvas snapped taunt in the wind, the sound unnerving. Open bags of garbage and personal belongings cluttered front yards and were spread throughout the streets, sidewalks, and in random places like outside of the car wash. Many of the homes and businesses were blackened shells, burnt to the ground. The ones that weren't, had shattered windows, missing and broken doors. She felt overwhelmed by the carnage, the deserted city a wasteland of death and destruction. This couldn't be real. She had to be dreaming.

Astra remembered hearing about the hydro out-ages from the news reports during the second year of the pandemic. By year four, news coverage had become intermittent and was rarely up to date, the same frightful stories circulating over and over. Then the Internet died, followed by the power then the taps went dry. Any well water had to be boiled if you hadn't been lucky enough to have stocked-piled years' worth of bottled water before the looters and hoarders had gotten everything. She was grateful her parents had thought ahead, thought of everything including the underground power generators, solar panels, and water that was pumped from a large well stored in the underground double-reinforced con-crete water tanks. They had invested their life sav-ings into the bunker. She and Jude had been lucky to have hot showers and meals when the population around them was starving and dying from the virus.

At times, Astra felt a heaviness, a pang of unspeak-able guilt weighing down on her chest. They had sur-vived when so many hadn't only because her parents had the knowledge and foresight to be prepared. She didn't think even her parents could have foreseen how bad it really was going to be.

Clouds drifted across the sun and cast sharp shadows against the city's remains. Astra prayed her sister was still alive. She had to be. She wondered what Hope looked like after five years. Once they had the antibiotics, they would head to The Closure and find her. After everything they had been through, Astra's determination was stronger ever. She would find Hope. She wouldn't stop searching until she did. Movement from the back seat caught her attention and her gaze lifted to the rear-view mirror. Jude was awake, his eyes glazed. "How are you feeling?"

He gave her a bleak smile and sat up slowly. "Like I was hit by a tornado. I think I'm running a fever."

She reached behind the seat and pressed her hand against his forehead. His skin was scolding hot to touch. "You're burning up." Worry gnawed at her. Fever meant infection. Untreated infection equaled death. He needed antibiotics.

As if reading her mind, he reassuringly squeezed her shoulder. "Hey, I'll be okay. After l get some anti-biotics into me, I'll be as good as new. We're almost at the pharmacy."

"What if the pharmacy was burned down? What about the safe?"

"Trust me, the safe is well hidden. It will be there."

Astra hoped he was right otherwise they would have to look elsewhere. She knew there was a very slim chance of finding any antibiotics anywhere else. The thought worried her and made her feel on edge.

Jude looked out the window with wide eyes. "Win-nipeg sure doesn't look like it used to. It's worst than I imagined. I'm not sure what I expected but it sure isn't this."

Her stomach tightened at the bleak landscape. "It's really bad. I can't believe it. We can't be the only two people alive. I haven't seen one person. Only dogs and cats." She glanced at Raider curled up sleeping, happy he was safe. "The animals, they're so skinny and hungry. There's so much suffering. It makes me want to cry."

"Please, don't cry." He squeezed her shoulder again. "It's out of our hands. There's nothing we can do for them. They'll sort it out, their way."

Astra knew he was right, but it didn't make it any easier. She felt defeated, angry, and sad. They barely had enough food to feed themselves and Raider today, let alone tomorrow. Astra tried not to think about it and clenched the steering wheel with both hands.

Steering the truck onto Pioneer Ave, they drove past the ruins of the Lucky Leaf Supermarket where her family frequently shopped. The store had been stripped clean. Many rows of windowless buildings were tagged with graffiti. Some buildings were riddled with bullet holes and looked like a war had taken place. A half a block up on the right, the rectangular red and blue Waverly Family Pharmacy sign came into view. She took her foot off the gas pedal and coasted to a stop in front of the store. A heap of shattered glass lay on the sidewalk where the large glass plate window and glass door used to be. Relieved the two-storey building hadn't been burned down, she shut off the engine and did up the windows. Her gaze shifted across the street to the sprawling Eternal Flame Funeral Home. Hundreds of coffins stacked high on the front and side lawn made her muscles tense. Astra dragged her focus back to the store.

"At least they didn't torch the pharmacy. Looks like they burned down pretty much everyone else," Jude said with a bit of pep in his voice as he stared at his family's storefront.

She peered at the building and remembered all of the times she'd met him here after school with their friends. They were happy times. Times long gone. A scrawny black cat zoomed in front of the truck and disappeared behind an overloaded dumpster on the other side of the street. Raider's ears perked up. His tail beat excitedly against her arm at the sight of the feline. "If I open the door, I'm sure he'll take off after that cat."

"I can make a leash. There's some rope in the toolbox. " He opened the door and climbed out.

Astra got out and shoved the keys into her pocket still shocked by what the city looked like. After Jude made a leash out of braided yellow rope, she looped the rope over Raider's head then wrapped the self-made handle securely around her wrist. The dog jumped out of the truck and sat patiently beside her waiting for her to put on her mask and gloves. Jude handed her a Glock 19. Astra took the handgun, as if it was a natural thing to do, praying she wouldn't have to use the weapon. While holding the shotgun in one hand, Jude grabbed the backpack with the first aid kit in it from the back of the truck. Glass cracked and popped under their feet as they walked inside of the pharmacy.

CHAPTER FIVE

The first thing Jude noticed was the ATM was missing next to the prescription pickup counter. It wasn't as if money would be of any use. Not anymore. As he glanced around the barren pharmacy, he made up his mind not to tell Astra how ill he felt, how badly the chills had set in, or how much his body ached with fever. It would only make her worry more. There was another problem, one he couldn't shake. He was sure someone had been watching them when they were outside. It wasn't his imagination. He had felt a set of eyes locked on his back and they weren't friendly. "I think someone was watching us."

Astra stopped and looked at him. "When?"

"When we were putting on our masks."

"Are you sure?"

"I think so." He spotted a glimpse of fear in her eyes. He hated upsetting her. They'd already been through so much.

"We'd better hurry and get the antibiotics. Where's the safe?"

"In my father's office." He pointed to the stairs to the second floor. Pushing one of the overturned white metal display shelves swept clean of medications out of their way, Jude wondered if people who had been infected had used some of the high-powered prescription pain medications that had been available in the pharmacy to end their lives in desperation or maybe salvation. He kept moving and shook the gut-wrenching thought from his mind.

On the second floor in the narrow hallway, the heavy metal lock had been cut off the door to the storage room where his father had kept extra stock for the store. Jude peered inside. Empty shelves greeted him and a half dozen empty cardboard boxes.

Astra sighed. "Looks like they took everything."

He frowned and shook his head in disgust unable to digest that this was their world now. A world with nothing.

"Wait." Astra pointed toward the back wall. "What's that on the floor in the corner behind that big box?"

Jude walked into the room, pushed some of the boxes out of the way, and lifted the last one. He bent down and picked up the large bag of potato chips. His mouth watered. Unable to remember the last time they had any junk food to eat, he held the bag up in the air like he'd found gold. "They left us something."

Passing the chips to Astra, her eyes lit up, and a smile curved her lips. Raider sat next to his leg, drooling. Astra glanced down at the dog. "Don't worry. You'll get some."

When Jude exited the room, Astra's face formed into a frown. "What's wrong?"

"Your back. You're bleeding through the bandage. It needs to be changed.

"Come on. We'll do it in the office."

At the end of the hallway, he pushed open the door to his father's office. The room had been pillaged and almost bare. His father's computer was gone, the telephone and the large landscape picture of a sailboat that always hung behind the desk. Business papers were tossed about on the floor and covered the desk. His father's prized trophy he'd won six years ago for 'Winnipeg's Business of the Year' sat broken in half at his feet. Anger boiled over. His father had worked twenty years to win the award, just tossed out like garbage. Jude kicked the pieces of the trophy aside, wishing they could wake up from this bad dream.

While Astra unpacked and prepared the medical supplies to redress his wound, Jude slid the large wooden desk across the floor directly under the air conditioning vent in the back corner of the room. Grunting, he climbed up onto the desk and removed the vent. Reaching inside, pain lanced through his spine and made him wince. Determined, he stretched his fingertips and searched for the metal personal safe. When he touched cold metal, he pulled the safe closer to him and retrieved the rectangular box. Sitting down on the desk, he punched his birthdate into the manual keypad. The lid clicked open. Inside, he found a bottle of generic antibiotics containing one hundred pills, a large roll of fifty and one-hundred-dollar bills, two small bottles containing a clear liquid, and a box of syringes. He looked at the label on one of the bottles and it read; Curaxin. It was the vaccine produced by Pharmova. He couldn't believe it. Relief relaxed his muscles. According to the last news reports they had watched on TV, the mRNA-V2 vaccine was ninety-eight percent effective against the XBU virus. They wouldn't have to worry now if Astra's parents were wrong about the virus burning itself out.

Astra peered over his shoulder. "Are the antibiotics in there?"

"Yep. And this." He handed her one of the vaccine bottles.

Astra studied the bottle and her eyes widened. "This is the vaccine."

Unscrewing the top of the antibiotics, he popped

two of the 500mg tablets in his mouth and downed the medication dry. "I bet the vaccine had probably shipped early to the pharmacies before the government tried to begin to vaccinate what was left of the population."

"We know how well that worked out," Astra said, still focused on the bottle. Unfortunately, they did, had witnessed it on the TV and on the Internet. Approximately, sixteen to eighteen billion doses of Curaxin had been needed to inoculate every single person on the planet. Between manufacturing problems, distribution glitches, and not enough medical personnel at the mass vaccination sites to administer it, it quickly became a losing battle. A large number of doses of the vaccine had even been stolen from military storage sites in various countries then sold on the black market at outrageous prices only the mega-rich could afford. Even worse, some opportunistic people envisioned a money-making opportunity by selling fake vaccines to desperate people, while the poorest countries with the weakest infrastructure never received a single bottle of the life-saving vaccine.

Astra's brows drew together. "I don't understand. Why didn't your parents use it?"

Jude fought through the wave of grief snarling inside him. If his parents had been vaccinated, they'd probably be alive. It didn't make sense. Suddenly, the dog's tail went ramrod straight and he growled. Jude hopped to his feet and seized his shotgun leaning against the wall. Raider kept growling a deep, low warning.

Astra grabbed the leash, yanked him back, and snatched her gun sitting on top of the backpack.

The stairs creaked.

Jude's heartbeat stuttered in his chest. His gaze flickered from Astra and then to the doorway.

"Someone's here," Astra whispered, clutching her gun.

"Stay right beside me." The stairs creaked again followed by heavy footsteps. Jude's body hummed with adrenaline. He jerked the gun up and aimed it in the direction of the doorway. A lengthy shadow appeared in the hallway and slinked slowly along the wall like a ghost. Fear pooled in Jude's gut.

* * *

A scrawny man with a scraggly beard and grime caked on his face loomed in the doorway. His rifle was aimed at them, his expression stone cold. He stared at Astra for several long moments, sizing her up.

Her body went rigid. Raider barked frantically.

The man glared at the dog, his dark eyes narrow

slits. "Shut the hell up."

The dog stopped barking but kept growling.

The man took a menacing step forward them, his oversized navy t-shirt and blue jeans stained and ripped.

Jude gestured at him with the barrel of the shotgun. "Stay right where you are. Not an inch closer."

The stranger stopped and gave them a dirty look. His penetrating gaze swept the room and landed on the vaccine bottles. "Give me the backpack and what-ever else you got over there on the desk."

Astra gripped the gun tighter.

"That's not going to happen," Jude said. "How about you just turn around and leave."

"How about I shoot the girl?" He licked his peeling lips then glared at the dog. "Or the mutt?"

Astra's swallowed down the stinging acid creeping up the back of her throat. No one was going to hurt Raider. There was no way she was going to give in to the stranger's demands. Her heartbeat pumped faster. He wasn't going to take anything from them. Terrified he would shoot them, in a last-ditch effort Astra tried to talk some sense into him. "If you agree to leave, we'll give you the bag of potato chips we found. That's all we have. Please. We don't want any trouble."

The man's hateful brown eyes lit at the mention of the chips, then the light extinguished. "What's yours is mine. That's how it works around here."

Out of the corner of her eyes, she noticed Jude shivering. He was getting weaker by the minute. The wound in his back was bleeding through the dressing again. Fear wove through her as she watched him struggle to keep the shotgun held up and aimed at the man.

"Take the deal and walk away," Jude murmured, his voice strengthening. "That's your only choice here."

"Give me everything you got," the man snarled. "I'm not asking again."

Astra knew he wasn't going to accept her offer or back down. He was as desperate as they were. Her pulse thudded in her throat. She wasn't going to wait for him to kill them or Raider. The man was ruthless. It was in his eyes. It was them or him. Astra tightened her fingers on the gun and refused to think about what she was about to do.

A gunshot cracked. The pungent smell of nitroglycerin, sawdust, and graphite swirled in the air. Blood seeped from the man's chest and left a wet stain, fanning out across his t-shirt. He staggered backward then his rifle dropped and hit the floor with a thud. He clutched his chest with both hands, his gaze ferocious. "You bitch!" His eyes darted to his gun.

Astra couldn't let him get to his gun. She braced herself and squeezed off another shot. The man fell to his knees, clutching his abdomen. When he screamed out in pain, her blood curdled. The scream didn't sound close to being human. Bleeding profusely, his lips tightened into a thin line, and he rose back up onto one knee. He stretched out an arm toward his rifle. He wasn't going to stay down.

She fired again. This time, the bullet caught him above his left eye and knocked him backward. His body twitched for what seemed like forever then finally stilled. Slowly lowering the gun to her side Astra gasped. Tears rolled down her cheeks and she shook uncontrollably as if her body had a mind of its own.

Jude's hand touch hers. He took the gun from her and placed it on the desk behind him. "It's over."

The shocking realization of what she had done made her breath quicken. "Oh, God, I killed him." If her parents were still alive, they would never have forgiven her for such a cold-blooded act. She was a killer. Gasping in huge gulps of air, she forced herself to breathe. Then she doubled over and threw up.

When she was done, Jude handed her a bottle of water. "He would have killed us, no doubt about it."

Taking a drink to help flush the bitter taste from her mouth, she had never considered herself a violent person. The world changed and so did she. "It still doesn't make it okay."

"I know but things are different now. Self-preservation comes with some scary rules: eliminate everyone you meet and take everything they have. I doubt this will be the only time we'll have to defend ourselves against other survivors. Everything we have is of value to someone else and vice versa. We have to remember that."

The conversation felt wrong on so many levels. The world was an ugly, hateful place. Astra felt numb inside. She couldn't believe she killed the man. It would always be her and Jude against someone who wanted to take the little they had. They'd always be looking over their shoulder to stay alive.

He wrapped his arms around her and held her. "You'll get through this like you've gotten through everything else."

Astra sagged against him and felt his body react to hers. She closed her eyes and buried her head in his shoulder not wanting to let go until she felt the searing heat emitting from his body. He felt as hot as a furnace. Worry resurfaced and she opened her eyes. "You're really burning up."

"I feel like crap." He released her and sat on the edge of the desk.

Pain and exhaustion registered on his face and

made the dark circles under his eyes more prominent. Astra needed him healthy, at one hundred percent, especially if they ended up having another problem with a survivor. She just wanted to leave the pharmacy, forget about what happened and go home but they were only a few blocks away from The Closure and minutes away from finding Hope. There was no going back. There wasn't a do-over. What happened, happened. Finding her sister would be her only saving distraction, the driving force that would help her forget the unforgivable thing she had done.

CHAPTER SIX

As Jude steered the truck onto the Arlington Street bridge, he peered through the iron trusses at the silent Canadian Pacific Railway yard below. Long lines of trains sat on the rails, the desolate landscape forgotten, ravaged by a destructive and deadly past. There was still no mistaking the faint smell of death in the air. Astra sat quietly in the passenger seat, feeding one of the bags of beef jerky they had left to the dog. Jude didn't think she had it in her to kill, the shock and panic evident by her reaction. She hadn't flinched. Not once. He understood how difficult it must have been for her to do. The last time he'd seen her this upset was when she had learned her parents had been infected with the virus. Jude couldn't imagine how she felt shooting another human being. Unfortunately, he had a feeling eventually he would find out. They had been forced to grow up, toughen up, not by choice, but by necessity to do whatever it took to survive. If it meant they had to kill, he would have to be okay with that. They both would. What other choice did they have? It was the wild west, everyone for themselves. Jude hoped she could forgive herself for something out of her control. He would have killed the stranger himself, but he was too weak, dizzy, his vision blurring in and out from the high fever. If he had taken the shot and missed, the man would have killed all of them. Astra was protecting them, her family. He hoped she would eventually see it that way.

"You should have had more to eat besides the protein bar." She handed him the last strip of beef jerky.

"I'm fine." He popped the meat in his mouth and savored the rich smoky beef flavor. "What about you?"

"I'll have some nuts in a bit." She crumpled the empty bag into a ball and tossed it on the floor at her feet.

Jude was grateful his father had left the bottles of Curaxin in the safe. He just wished his parents had used it for themselves. Before leaving the pharmacy, Astra had put a fresh bandage on his wound. Afterward, he'd downed a couple more of the antibiotics with a full bottle of water. He didn't feel great. His body felt weak, his gut a swirling mess from the medication and not eating enough. He was sure his fever had gone down a tiny bit since the chills weren't coming as often as they had been.

A few minutes later, he parked the truck behind the ruins of a burnt semi-collapsed fast-food restaurant.

He turned off the ignition and grasped Astra's hand, her palm warm against his. "I don't want you to get your hopes up. Your sister may not be at The Closure. A lot of time has gone by, a lot has happened in five years."

She lowered her head and stared at her hands. "I know there's a chance she might be somewhere else or even dead. I can't give up on her. Not yet. I promised my father." Astra lifted her chin and looked at him. "I won't give up until I know for sure what's happened to her. Hope deserves that."

He squeezed her hand, understanding her need for answers, to find out what happened to her last family member. He wanted so much for Hope to be alive for Astra's sake. Jude wasn't sure she was strong enough to deal with another emotional blow. "I'm going to take the Glock with me and keep it concealed. You should have a weapon too. We'll hide the supplies to play it safe."

She nodded in agreement. "Especially the weapons and the ammunition."

"And the vaccine," Jude added. "We might be able to trade the vaccine for something we need."

"Maybe."

He released her hand and got out of the truck. A light breeze ruffled his hair and felt good against his skin.

Once they hid the supplies behind a washing machine in the collapsed building, they walked the half-block to what was known as The Closure, a spanning parcel of land owned by the Canadian government. When they reached the scientific sanctuary, a flock of birds flew overhead and soared high in the clear blue sky. There weren't any decaying human remains baking in the sun or trash in the parking lot in front of the pristine four-storey white structure like there was throughout the rest of the city. The building and grounds were enclosed, secured with a ten-foot chain-link fence topped with coiled barbed wire.

On the other side of the fence, Jude noticed two men talking, carrying green Canadian military issued C7A2 rifles. They were dressed in two-tone brown fatigues and wore matching camouflage cloth masks over their mouths and noses. Part of him was relieved to see them, the other, extremely cautious after what had happened at the pharmacy. It was hard to tell the good guys from the bad. He waved and yelled to get their attention. "Hey. We're looking for someone."

The men walked toward him. They didn't appear to be much of a threat until he noticed the men's grip tighten around their rifles. They stopped about three meters away from him. Jude averted his gaze to the shorter man with a long, thin face that didn't seem to match his body.

The man pulled out a hand-held no-contact thermometer from his belt. "Where did you two come from? The taller of the two asked. "We don't get any survivors showing up here anymore."

Jude wasn't about to tell them they'd been living underground for five years. He changed the subject. "Are you two military?"

The men looked at each other. Then the taller man gave a curt nod.

The hairs on Jude's arms stood up. He didn't believe the man. He remained alert and cautious. The words, 'trust no one', rolled through his mind. "We're trying to find someone. A girl. She was brought here at the beginning of the outbreak."

The men exchanged glances again.

Then the shorter man chuckled. "That was a long time ago. Many people have come and gone. I doubt she's still here."

Astra moved closer to the fence and clutched the leash. Raider stood by her side wagging his tail. "We just want to see if she is. She's my sister." Astra pulled the crumpled photograph out of her pocket, unfolded it, and pointed to Hope. "Please. I need to find her."

The tall man gestured with his hand to his buddy. "You had better check them."

"Get right up at the fence. We need to record your

temperature. No one gets in with a fever," the short man said, looking perturbed as if they were wasting his time.

Jude's heart sank. He looked at Astra and saw the light drain from her eyes. They did as they were told and met the man at the fence, hoping the men would understand and let them in.

He pointed the thermometer at Astra's forehead first. A minute later, the device beeped. He looked at the small screen and then at the taller man. "She's clear." The man stepped in front of Jude and repeated the process. "This one's got a fever. A hundred and two."

"You need to leave," the tall man said in a stern tone as he stepped back. "You're infected."

Astra shook her head. "No, please. He doesn't have the virus. He's running a fever because the wound in his back is infected." She glanced at Jude. "Show him."

The pain in his back was constantly throbbing and burning, but he ignored it. He turned and lifted his t-shirt, thankful, he'd concealed the Glock in the front of his pants.

"Looks like you got into a bit of a scuffle with a survivor, eh?"

Jude lowered his shirt and faced him. "No. A tornado. We ran into one earlier on the way here."

The man's eyes widened. "That's some nasty shit. Where are you two coming from?"

Before Jude could answer, the tall man scratched his forehead and asked, "What have you got for us?"

Jude swallowed hard and played dumb. He knew what the men wanted. Anything they had. "What do you mean?"

"Like a token of appreciation for letting you in, you know, cash, jewelry, something of value," the tall man explained. "Ayden Webb wouldn't be happy if we let you in with a fever. Everything that happens here is reported to him."

Jude had no idea who Ayden Webb was and didn't care. They had waited five years, lived through the virus, and survived a tornado, they had to get inside to look for Hope so Astra could have some closure. He wasn't going to give up for her sake. He reached into one of his pant pockets and pulled out half of the money from the safe that he'd divided and left the other half in the glove box of the truck. He held up the bundle of bills. "Here's two thousand dollars. It's yours after you let us in."

The tall man's eyes went huge. He shot a nod to his buddy who reached in his pocket and pulled out a set of keys. "Go to the gate. We'll let you in."

* * *

The sun beat against Astra's back as she walked beside Jude and followed the men through the large parking lot. Her heartbeat sped up in anticipation. This was it. They were going to find her sister. Excitement built inside her chest. Astra stomped it down in case Hope wasn't here. She couldn't take another disappointment or loss. Exhaling a nervous breath, she shortened Raider's leash and quickened her step. "How many others are with you?"

The tall man asked, his eyes roaming the area behind them. "Did you bring any belongings with you?"

Jude shook his head. "It's just us. We don't have any belongings."

The shorter man eyed the dog. "What's his name?"

"Raider," Jude said.

He then stared at her. "You never mentioned where you're coming from."

Every nerve ending in Astra's body tingled and she lied. She would never reveal the location of the bunker. "A barn, south of here, up by Garden City." She didn't like the man's small talk, the way he was prying for information. Astra was beginning to think the men weren't who they claimed to be. "You mentioned someone by the name of Ayden Webb. Who is he? A scientist?"

The tall man's gaze connected with hers and his brows raised. "Lady, there aren't any scientists here.

Haven't been in a long time. Ayden Webb runs The Closure."

She and Jude looked at each other, confused.

The men stopped at a wooden barricade at the far end of the parking lot. The tall man turned to his pal. "Pat them down."

A shiver of fear coursed up Astra's spine. The guns!

The man ran his hands up and down Jude's body then lifted the front of his shirt. "No weapons are allowed inside." He confiscated the Glock and tucked it in his belt. He turned to Astra, his piercing eyes glued to her body. "You got anything you want to tell me about before I search you?"

Yeah. She didn't want his fat hands on her. He was giving her the creeps the way he was gawking at her. Astra lifted her tank-top just enough to retrieve the gun from the back of the waistband, pressed against the small of her back. She reluctantly handed him the Sig Saucer P226.

He took the weapon and kept staring directly at her. "Empty those pockets."

She put one hand on her hip and glared at him. Astra had enough of the way they were treating them. "Is this really necessary?"

The man's head moved slowly up and down. "You might have another weapon on you." He winked at

Jude. "She's a spitfire, isn't she?"

She could barely refrain from rolling her eyes. She reached into her pocket and retrieved the folded photograph she'd shown the men earlier. "See. It's a photograph."

Jude pulled out a handful of pills from his jeans pocket. "They're antibiotics, for the infection."

The tall man glanced at the pills, his gray eyes twinkling in the sunlight. "Keep them." He slapped Jude on his shoulder and caused him to flinch. "We don't want to see you getting sicker there, big boy." He turned to the short man. "Show them down to the camp. I'll let Webb know we have a couple of walk-ins. He'll be quite excited to have a couple of new-comers."

The last Astra had heard, all the scientists and other personnel were still located in the building because it was a secure government medical facility. She didn't understand what had happened.

Jude piped up before she had the chance to say any-thing. "What camp? I thought we were going inside the building."

"It is off-limits. The building is for Ayden Webb's use only. Survivors stay in the camp."

Why would one man need a whole building for himself? Astra had no idea what was going on, but the vibe coming from the man didn't feel right.

Something was off. She couldn't shake the horrible feeling they had walked into something much uglier, more dangerous than they had left on the outside of The Closure. Astra prayed she was wrong.

While the men escorted them to the back of the building and down a long semi-dark narrow tunnel, Jude held her hand. Anxiety sent her nerves on high alert. Through her mask, the strong scent of human waste invaded her nostrils. The putrid vile stink stung her eyes and made them water. As they approached the end of the passageway, she heard loud voices. Lots of them. The men stopped. Astra froze. Goosebumps rose on her arms.

Jude's hand slipped out of hers.

The tunnel opened into a sprawling outdoor tarped camp crammed with an obstacle course of run-down tents in assorted sizes, shapes, and shanty-like structures haphazardly slapped together with leftover building materials. Shopping carts, folding chairs, blankets, and belongings were scattered all over the place. The foul stench of urine was thick in the air. Weary-looking teenagers wandered about. Some huddled together in small groups and were playing board games. Others were walking around looking lost, dazed. The living conditions were deplorable. The camp reminded her of the images she had seen on the Internet of Skid Row in Los Angeles. The sight tore at her soul and all she could think about was her sister.

"What is this?" Jude asked, his blue eyes wide with shock. "It looks like a prison camp."

Their escort held out his arm as if he was showing off a prize on a game show. "Welcome to The Closure."

Cold drove through Astra's bones and her knees trembled. She stared at him in confusion. "This can't be right. The children—my sister was brought here by the government to be tested to see if she was immune to the virus. I don't understand." Her voice trailed off.

The man looked at her. "The second coming of Christ happened. Lots of people died. The kids grew up."

She shivered involuntarily. The camp was filthy and chaotic. Dogs and cats roamed freely, racing around chasing each other and doing their business. Distress flashed in the eyes of some of the teenagers who dared to meet her gaze. Astra scanned the compound for females her sister's age with auburn hair. She didn't see any.

Jude's eyes darkened and matched the tone of his voice. "How many are here?"

"At last count, one hundred and twelve," the man replied.

So many questions plowed through Astra's mind. She wasn't sure where to begin. "What about food? Who feeds them?"

He kept his eyes straight ahead. A few seconds passed before the man said anything. "They have to fight for food. A battle of the strongest."

Astra sucked in a startled breath. "What are you talking about?"

"What the hell kind of place is this?" Jude shook his head. "They'd have a better chance on the outside than here."

The man glanced at him, and his voice soured. "That's a matter of opinion. Webb thinks differently." He glanced at his wristwatch. "The food lottery begins in two hours. Whichever group wins the most fights will receive extra food for their group for the week as well as a few other perks that our teams have brought in. The lottery is an incentive, to teach them how to physically prepare for life on the outside. There are no free rides, not in here."

She drew a tense breath to steady her nerves and said, "They're children for heaven's sake."

The man shrugged. "They're old enough. Most are seventeen or eighteen now. They must prepare so they are ready for the outside. The apocalypse is the second coming of Christ to recycle the world to a clean slate. These kids were brought to this location for a reason. It was God's will. They are the holy children of light and will be the ones who will rule the future of mankind. They need guidance, discipline, and extensive training before they can be sent out to rebuild the world."

Astra stifled a laugh and dismissed the ridiculous notion. "You're being brainwashed by this Ayden Webb person. Do you really believe that garbage?"

He gave her a sharp look, his tone abrupt. "We all believe. We're dedicated to God's mission. The old world was run by the devil and look where we are now." He took a breath and glanced at Jude's mask. "The kids are immune to the virus. The government tested all of them when they were here."

It was clear the guy couldn't or wasn't able to grasp he was being manipulated by a religious fanatic who was mentally disturbed. "What happened to the government workers and the scientists?" Jude asked, looking as worried as she felt.

"Most of them ended up infected and died. Others left, thinking it was better on the outside. They left the kids to fend for themselves. It's a good thing Ayden Webb took over when he arrived."

Astra couldn't believe what she was hearing. Their government had abandoned the kids, leaving them to fend for themselves. Most of them had been eleven or twelve years old at the time. If Hope was here, she must have been so scared, still is, living like this for years. Astra was convinced the man was totally off his rocker and belonged locked up in a padded room along with Ayden Webb. Some of the survivors appeared so skinny she fought to hold back the tears glazing over her vision.

"Have you two been vaccinated?" The man asked, changing the subject.

She and Jude looked at each other and nodded at the same time. "Keep the masks on anyway. Better safe than sorry."

"How many have died since the government left?" Astra asked, totally dumbstruck. "There have been some, the weak ones, taken up to the sky. Webb says they died because they weren't cut out to rule mankind. Only the strong ones are."

"When you're practically starving half of them, no wonder some have died."

Struck by the terrible revelation, Astra couldn't listen to any more of this lunacy. She had to find her sister and leave this dreadful place. Retrieving the photograph from her pocket, she grabbed Jude's arm and they walked away.

Jude shook his head. "I've never seen anything like this. They're preying on those kids"

"It's a cult. A sect". Another thought punched her in the stomach with chilly clarity. "They have no intention of letting us leave, are they?"

"It doesn't look that way. We need to stay calm and focused. If Hope is here, we'll find her and get away from this place. We need a plan. It's going to be tricky." He gestured with his head. "See the guards positioned around the perimeter?"

She had been so busy listening to the man's brain-sick talk, she hadn't noticed the men dressed in camouflage shirts and pants holding rifles at the back fence stacked with two-foot-high barbed wire. Astra counted four guards and she cursed under her breath.

CHAPTER SEVEN

As the clouds thickened and blotted out the sun, Jude popped two pills into his mouth and swallowed them. Sitting on a small grassy patch away from everyone else, he spotted Astra stopping some of the adolescents and showing them the photograph of Hope. She wanted to look for her sister alone. Of course, he had protested, not that it did him any good. He had learned it was pointless to argue with her. Out of the corner of his eye, he watched a horde of rats skitter one by one along the bottom of a nearby decrepit tent and scurry inside. His heart beat suddenly faster. It was hard to think, witnessing the undeniable misery, the way despair curved some of the teenager's shoulders.

He knew this wasn't their fight to save them. They couldn't save everyone. There was no denying the living conditions were cruel, but so was the post-apocalyptic environment on the other side of the barbed wire. Jude had noticed the numerous rusted fire barrels scattered throughout the camp. Were the teenagers forced to live outside in the winter too? With summer coming, the adolescents would swelter in the humidity and heat. He shut his eyes and blocked out an alarming scream coming from somewhere deep within the camp. He couldn't imagine what it was like at night and didn't want to find out. There had to be something better than living like this. If the kids were outside of The Closure, they would have their choice of shelter and could hunt for food, not fight for it.

They would either make it or they wouldn't. It was a fifty-fifty chance for everyone who survived. Pre-packaged processed food was more than scarce. Whether Astra liked it or not, when they returned home, they would have to hunt rabbits, squirrels, and catch fish. It was something she would have to come to grips with no matter how she felt about eating anything with a face. Hunt or starve. It was their new reality.

Ayden Webb and his followers were delusional, the locked-up-kind-of-delusional. From what Jude had read about cults long before the virus, their leaders were narcissistic, charismatic, craved status and power and that made them unpredictable. By the sounds of it, Ayden Webb was both deranged and dangerous. There was no such thing as the second coming of Christ or holy children of light. The UXB virus had been injected into the wild by accident, a devastating event of epic proportions that no one could have predicted. The mess they were in had nothing to do with God. After what they had witnessed during the past five years, God no longer existed in his mind. If he did, he would never have allowed this to happen in the first place.

They were in a predicament, as his mother used to say. He wished his father was here. His father was a natural problem solver and he'd know what to do. Jude had to figure a way to get them out and back to the security of the underground bunker. His father had taught him to always be prepared. He opened his eyes and slid his fingers inside his right boot, felt the switchblade and lighter he'd duct-taped to the leather and the truck keys stuffed in his sock after he had hidden the supplies.

His eyes traveled to the pristine government building looming to the right in the shadows. It looked out of place stuck in the middle of all the doom and gloom. A lunatic was inside its walls while kids suffered for the sake of some preposterous end-of-the-world ideology. Jude blew out a long breath and felt a sudden hatred for a man he had never met. There appeared to be four guards plus the two men they'd encountered when they first arrived. He was lying to himself if he thought he could get them out of this mess himself. He had a switchblade and no gun. But he had to try.

Time crawled by and fatigue crept into his limbs.

Jude stretched out his legs and leaned back on his elbows, watching Astra talking to a brown-skinned teenager holding a soccer ball. He wondered if there was some sort of hierarchy with the teenagers within the camp like there was in prison. It would make sense with so many people crammed into one place, trapped.

He watched Raider race between the shelters, chasing a medium-sized brown dog as two girls ran after them, laughing. The sight made him sad, reminding him of the past, growing up. The memories of the outbreak stabbed at his mind and had splintered somewhat over the years. Maybe he had blocked them out not wanting to relive his last conversation with his parents or the helplessness he had felt, knowing he couldn't save them. Everyone who had survived the virus had to have PTSD. He couldn't forget the sleepless nights, the terrifying nightmares, or how many countless times he had woken up in an icy cold sweat, fighting to convince himself he was safe.

A sound caused him to look over his shoulder. The short man who had escorted them into the camp came into view. Well-cut blond short hair dissolved almost white around his face.

"Thought you could use this." The man handed him a bottle of water.

Jude sat up and took the bottle, grateful for a drink. "Thanks." Quick brown eyes studied him, staring.

"Has your girl found her sister?" Jude swallowed a big gulp of water, unnerved by the man's cool stare.

"Not yet." He paused and wondered if Hope had ever been outside of the camp. "Tell me more about Ayden Webb."

"There's not much to tell. He was an infantry soldier, CAF. He saw a lot of combat action back during the invasion of Afghanistan. When he returned home, he joined the Aquarian Church of the Divine, doing God's work then was anointed the Savior of Salvation. We're grateful he's here to guide us. He looks after all of us."

Jude could barely speak. His gaze shifted to his surroundings, and he wanted to laugh out loud but stopped himself. "Doesn't look like he's doing a great job."

"Again, that's a matter of opinion." A level of irritation crept into the man's tone. "Webb thinks differently. He channels the voice of God and ensures that the Devil Walkers don't get inside the camp."

Jude raised his eyebrows, wondering what the man meant. He'd always been a level-headed, rational person but the man's nutty talk was wearing on his nerves. "Devil Walkers? Are you serious?"

He sat down next to Jude and placed his rifle beside him on the grass. His face showed no emotion. Not even a blink. "Devil Walkers are the unchosen, the unfit, who live in the streets. It's them versus us. Over the years, they've tried to find creative ways to get into the camp. It happens less and less now as more of them die off."

The word, bizarre, was the only word that came to mind. Jude wasn't sure how to respond. The guy was a special kind of kooky if he believed what Ayden Webb was telling him. He took another drink of water and hesitated before asking, "What's your name?"

"Todd Jennings."

"How'd you end up here?"

The man's demeanor relaxed ever so slightly. "I've been here all along. I used to clean out the test animal's cages in the CL2 lab." He pulled out a long blade of grass and fiddled with it between his fingers. "I was lucky enough to be inoculated long before the vaccine became available to the public. I figured staying here was the safest choice."

Jude wondered if the man knew Astra's parents or had perhaps met them at some point. He had to admit he was somewhat surprised by the man's reply. Todd seemed well-spoken, educated, and sure of himself. It was hard to understand how he had become a devout believer of Ayden Webb's insane dribble. Maybe it was true. Everyone needed something to believe in, especially in times like this. "The government abandoned you, like the kids."

"Who could blame them amidst the pandemonium to cleanse the sins of mankind?"

"Webb's just using you, pushing his agenda. What he's telling you isn't true. It's all made up," Jude said, hoping to get the man to listen to rationality.

"Jesus Christ and his disciples were also persecuted for their beliefs. In time, you and your girl will believe and become dedicated to the mission like we all have."

Astra had been right. They weren't going to be allowed to leave. Jude wasn't deterred. They were leaving one way or another. "We aren't staying. We're here to find a family member and then we'll be on our way."

Todd climbed to his feet and scooped up his weapon. "The food lottery begins soon." He squared his shoulders and shot him another cold stare. "Dissent will not be tolerated."

Jude looked up at him and noted the threat in his voice.

* * *

With the photograph clutched in her hand, Astra walked between two tents with gaping holes on the side and bit down on her lower lip. She couldn't fathom how anyone could allow such suffering. They were just kids. In her mind, for years, she had imaged she had already found Hope and they were together, happy. The longer she searched the camp, the less optimistic she was becoming. She walked up to a girl who looked about the same age as her sister, sitting cross-legged on the ground, staring off into space. Astra noticed the purple and yellow bruises on the girl's knuckles. A few feet away, a boy with long black hair tied back in a ponytail was shadowboxing, his fists fiercely punching the air.

Astra crouched beside the girl and held out the photograph. "I'm looking for someone. Have you seen her? Her name is Hope. She has long, red hair like mine."

The girl's eyes met hers briefly. "I'm scared."

Astra's heart broke. "I know you are. What's your name?"

The girl was hesitant for a second then said, "Stephanie."

"I'm Astra."

The girl's shoulder's sunk and her head lowered. "I didn't want to fight again. I hurt her. I was so hungry. I had to win the food lottery. I'm her best friend. How could I have hurt her?"

Astra's heart skipped a beat. "Stephanie, who did you hurt?"

A moment of tense silence passed. "Hope. I hurt her. I didn't mean to."

Her sister was alive! Astra's heart sped up at the news. "Where is she?"

The girl continued to stare at the ground. "In our tent. We share it with two other girls."

A whirlwind of emotions drove through her, and Astra stood. "Show me, please, Stephanie. I'm her sister."

The girl looked at her confused. "She said you died from the virus."

"Take me to your tent. I haven't seen her in five years."

Stephanie finally got up and she frowned. "I'm sorry I hurt her. I didn't want to."

Astra put an arm around her shoulder and could tell the girl felt terrible about what she had done. "You were forced to fight. You didn't have a choice."

"He told us we're the holy children of light and we must show him we are strong enough to bear the weight of existence." "Believe me. He's lying to you, to everyone."

The girl stared at her blankly for a few seconds with puzzlement written across her face. "He tricked us?"

Astra nodded. "He did. In the worst possible way."

"I don't want to fight again. I can't." She pointed in the direction of a large black tent to the right mere yards away. "Our tent is behind there. It's the big red round one."

* * *

Astra's heart hammered. Outside of the tent, she closed her eyes, said a little prayer, and braced herself for the worst. Lifting the tent's flap, she ducked inside and froze. Hope!

Her sister was on her side curled up on a filthy mattress with her hair matted with sweat against her face. Her left eyelid was purplish-black and swollen shut. She had a fat bottom lip and contusions on her cheek. Her gaze snapped to Hope's swollen and bruised hands. If it wasn't for her red hair and the jagged scar on her right knee from when she had fallen off her bicycle when she was six, Astra wasn't sure she would have recognized her. She had never seen such senseless cruelty. She fell to her knees beside the mattress and choked back a strangled sob. "Hope, can you hear me? It's Astra."

Silence hung in the air. Hope finally turned her head and searched her face. "I thought for sure I was dreaming. It really is you."

She ran her hand over her sister tangled hair and felt increasingly frightened. "Look what they have done to you."

"I thought you had died. Oh, my God. I've missed you so much." She exhaled heavily and her eye glossed over with wetness. "Mommy and daddy are gone, aren't they?"

Years of wondering if Hope was alive hit Astra full force. Her sister had been forced to fend for herself since the age of twelve. Astra couldn't stop the tears from flowing. She didn't try. Her vision blurred and she kept blinking to focus. "They're gone. They passed away from the virus at the beginning of the outbreak after you were brought to The Closure. I promised I would find you and bring you home."

Tears trickled down Hope's cheek. "I didn't get to say goodbye to them."

"I know. I'm so sorry, sis."

"It's not your fault. The government, they brought us here. They treated us well and fed us regularly. Then a lot of them died, others left. Ayden Webb showed up and he made us fight. I am so hungry."

Her sister's struggle was more than Astra could bear and she couldn't stop crying. "You need medical attention."

Hope shook her head. "I'll be okay. I'm just sore. They won't help us."

"We're going to get you out here. Do you hear me? Jude is here. He'll get us home."

Hope licked her lips and held out a hand. "Jude's here? I always liked him. He's a good guy."

She couldn't believe how much her sister had matured. "You've grown up so much. You're taller than I am." Astra gently held her hand careful not to hurt her. "A girl by the name of Stephanie told me she did this to you."

"Please, don't be mad at her. She's been my only friend, my best friend. She did what was expected of her. They would have killed her if she had refused to fight in the food lottery."

Another sickening thought struck Astra and she nearly choked on her words. "Has anyone hurt you, you know, like in any other way?"

"No. I'm fine." Astra breathed a small sigh of relief and couldn't wait to get Hope home. "The food lottery starts soon. I need to get up. I have to fight. We need the extra food otherwise my group will go hungry for another week. We're already so weak."

"Do they not feed you anything?"

"Only a bowl of watered-down oatmeal or whatever else they find but only once a day."

Ayden Webb was starving them. Astra understood how difficult it was to find prepackaged food. It was a desperate situation but there were other options. There were still chickens, cows, pigs, and the Red River was filled with Walleye, Bass, and Northern

Pike. She doubted her sister had ever been outside of The Closure or knew what the world was like now. "Hope, you can't fight. You're injured. Your hands and your eye look pretty bad."

"You don't understand. I must. We're the chosen ones, the holy children of light. We must prove our strength and ability. Then we can leave."

Rage pulsed through her veins. Astra despised Ayden Webb. She couldn't imagine the horrors Hope had seen and endured. "I want you to listen to me carefully. You don't have to do anything you don't want to." She took a breath and kept her voice gentle yet firm. "Ayden Webb is not a leader, a prophet, a God, or chosen by God. He's mentally ill. Do you understand what I'm saying? He made it up to manipulate and control you using his own religious beliefs. He's made you and the others into his cult followers. You remember what daddy told you about cults?"

Hope stared at her for a long time, a faint recognition sparking in the back of her eye.

Astra's breathing sped up and she felt suddenly claustrophobic inside the tent's walls. "I'm going to help you up. We need to go and find Jude."

Her sister nodded then slowly sat up. When Astra clasped Hope's arm to help her to her feet, she noticed the number '93' handwritten on her sister's right wrist with a red magic marker.

"What's the number for?"

"Numbers are drawn during the Revelation Court the day before the lottery to see who will be fighting for their group. Two are chosen from each group. I'm in the group called, Prophecy. We have red numbers. Stephanie is with the Divine group. She has a black number. I've been chosen to fight today."

Astra's hands curled into fists. "You're not fighting, not if I can help it."

A single gunshot splintered the air coming from outside of the tent. They both stopped dead in mid-step. Seconds later, the camp fell silent. Astra held onto Hope's arm, and she lifted the canvas flap. They cautiously exited the tent.

Less than five yards away, Stephanie was flat on her back. Her dirty pink t-shirt was stained red in the center of her chest. Astra could tell she wasn't breathing.

Hope rushed to her friend and knelt in front of her. She steepled her hands in front of her and looked as if she was saying a prayer. Survivors swarmed around the body, gawking, and whispering to each other, their words drifting away in the air.

Someone in the camp yelled, "Murderer!"

The lone guard's eyes darted from face to face. "The

crazy girl tried to hit me over the head with a rock. She was so fast, she almost succeeded." He pointed with his rifle to a large rock next to his feet. "What else was I supposed to do? I had to defend myself."

Astra searched the crowd for Jude and found him. She grasped her sister by the elbow and steered through the camp away from the heartbreaking scene.

CHAPTER EIGHT

J ude adjusted his mask and stood next to Astra. A light breeze from the south blew through his hair. Hope sat a few yards away alone on the grass with her head lowered. "Is she okay?"

Astra glanced at him, her eyes puffy and rimmed with red from crying. "It's going to take some time. She's pretty beaten up and she lost her only friend. This place has broken her spirit. She's not the sister I remember. The government was supposed to protect her and the other kids."

Jude clenched his fists. The condition Hope was in ripped at his heart. If there had been something hard, like a wall, he probably would have punched it. Ayden Webb needed to be stopped. "Is she brainwashed like the others?"

"I don't think as much as most of them. Hope seems to understand she's been lied to." Astra bit down on her lower lip. "She's been chosen to fight in the food lottery."

Every muscle in his body tensed and Jude felt Astra's despair. He looked around to make sure one was close and lowered his voice. "I've got the knife in my boot and a lighter. I'm going to try to get a rifle from one of the guards. It's our only chance."

She shook her head. "It's too dangerous. There's too many of them."

"We don't have a choice. We have to try." Jude understood the risks. He rubbed his forehead and racked his mind for another solution. He couldn't come up with one. They needed a gun. Without one, there was no chance of escaping. His eyes skimmed the camp, the run-down shelters, and the four men pacing at the back fence holding their weapons. "If I can get one of the rifles, I can shoot the rest of them." He had hoped he could have gotten through to Todd, but the man was too far gone. A lost cause. If he had to kill him, he would.

Raider trotted by, tail wagging, and laid down beside Hope. He nuzzled her with his nose clearly aware of her distress. Hope placed her hand on the dog's head and her body language relaxed with each stroke of his fur.

"Looks like she's made a new friend," Astra said, with a trace of a smile in her eyes.

A male's loud voice bellowed and sounded as if it

was coming through a blowhorn. "The Savior of Salvation calls you! The Savior of Salvation calls you!"

Everyone in the camp stopped what they were doing and began to fall into a single line.

He and Astra exchanged glances.

"What's that all about?" Astra asked.

"It's the Call." Hope said over her shoulder. "It's time to gather in the basement for the Food Lottery." When she walked over to them, Raider followed.

"We have to stop this," Astra said. "She's in no condition to fight. What are we going to do?"

Jude remembered that Todd had the keys to the gate. Still trying to form a clear plan in his mind, he bent down and reached into his boot. Grabbing the knife, he quickly shoved it into his pocket, wishing it was the Glock instead. "Todd has the keys to the gate. We need to get them from him."

Hope's gaze searched his eyes. "I have to get in line." She went silent for a second. "If anything happens to me, promise you will take care of Astra. She's always loved you. I know you love her too."

His throat ran dry with fear. "Nothing is going to happen to you."

Astra snagged her sister's arm and tightened her hold. "Please, Hope. Don't fight. We'll do everything we can to protect you. We need time to come up with a plan."

"I can't." Hope wrenched her arm free. "They'll kill me or worse kill you and Jude. You saw what they did to Stephanie. They've done it before."

They had to figure this out. Hope couldn't give up. None of them could. It would destroy Astra if anything happened to her sister after they'd been reunited. He wasn't going to watch that happen. Jude put his hand on Hope's shoulder and his eyes met Astra's. "We stick together, no matter what. "The first chance I can get to kill one of the guards, I'm taking it."

"Please, be careful," Astra pleaded. "I can't lose you too."

"It's going to be okay." He took several breaths and glanced at Hope. "Do all the guards go to the basement for the food lottery?"

She nodded. "They place bets on the fights."

Astra's gaze held his and her skin went white.

His body stiffened. That explained why the men had been so happy to see the cash he had on him from the pharmacy. It still didn't make sense since money was useless. There was nothing to buy. Maybe they were saving it up to see what the future held.

Behind him, the distinctive click of a rifle being cocked snagged his attention. Jude turned to see

Todd standing yards away with his rifle directed at them. He let out a frustrated breath. The man was too far away for him to get his gun, an opportunity lost, diminishing the chance of escaping. They stared at each other for what felt like minutes. He'd had enough of the lunacy. Jude gritted his teeth. "This isn't going to end well. You can count on it."

"Your adversary the devil prowls around like a seething lion, seeking someone to devour." Todd's eyes hardened. "Get in line. It's time for the Savoir of Salvation to continue his important work."

Jude was so disturbed by Todd's reaction, he grabbed Astra's and Hope's hands and headed to the end of the line.

Minutes later, the guards chaperoned the group through the tunnel. The air carried a strange sense of anticipation and fear. On the other side, they entered through the side door of the building and headed down a flight of stairs lit by portable solar lights, leading to the lower level. Footsteps sounded like continuous thunder around him. As they walked through double open metal doors, Jude was sure they had entered Hell.

* * *

In the massive basement, Astra stared in disbelief at the larger-than-life hand-painted image on the wall behind a wooden stage of a man dressed in a white robe with a bald head and long beard. Portable solar lights and candles lit the space as harp music played softly coming from somewhere next to the bottom of stairs leading to an ornately decorated red velvet and gold throne. The throne reminder her of the catherdra in the Catholic church where she and Hope had attended Sunday school when they were growing up. They had to find a way out of the camp. She pointed to the image on the wall and a nervous shiver rippled under her skin. "That must be Ayden Webb."

"This is crazy, totally insane." Jude shook his head. "The sooner we get out of here, the better." His gaze fixed on Todd and the five other guards standing in front of the stage, gripping their guns.

The adolescents fanned out like obedient robots and began to fill the bleachers on each side of the room. Behind the seating areas, brightly colored painted rainbows stretched across the walls. A large handwritten sign was posted above each set of bleachers that read: Prophecy. Divine. The smell of fear, melted wax, and sweat penetrated her mask. Astra noticed one of the guards holding a video camera. She looked at Hope. "They videotape the food lottery?"

Her sister pushed a lock of auburn hair out of her eyes. "Ayden Webb says the videos will be a permanent record for mankind to avoid damnation in the future."

"They bet on the kids and tape them." Anger rose in Jude's voice. "That's just sick." The whole situation was demented.

Astra eyed the door to the stairs leading to the tunnel. "We need a diversion."

"I think we need a couple of them," Jude said quietly.

Astra looked around the room then her gaze shifted to her sister. "Jude, your lighter. We can set Hope's sweater on fire." She twisted in the seat and pointed. "See all those cardboard boxes against the wall behind us?"

He glanced over his shoulder.

"Those are the boxes of food for the group that wins," Hope said. "There's clothes and blankets in them too."

Jude and Astra glanced at each other. Astra wasn't thrilled about setting the boxes on fire with everyone so hungry and suffering, including them. There was no other choice. "We burn them. While that's happening, Jude can look after Todd, get the gate key, and shoot the rest of the guards."

Jude nodded. "Then we go out the side door, up the stairs to the tunnel, unlock the gate and run like hell." He was silent for a minute, thinking. "It sounds pretty risky...but it might work."

"It will work, only if Hope doesn't have to fight first. Everyone will be busy watching the fight and the guards will be videotaping and placing their bets."

"What if Hope has to fight first?"

"Leave that to me. I have an idea. I'll keep Ayden Webb focused on me."

"It sounds like you've thought of everything."

"And everything that could go wrong," Astra said. "We can't worry about the what-ifs. We need to believe we can do this."

"What do you want me to do?" Hope asked.

"Take off your sweater and drop it behind you," Jude said. "I'll light it on fire and make sure the boxes go up in flames."

Her sister slipped off the sweater and dropped it behind her on the floor. "How do we know Todd will come back here?"

"We don't but there's a good chance he will since he's the closest to our bleacher. It doesn't matter. Any guard with a gun will do. I'll pretend I'm trying to put out the fire. Then once all the guards are dead, the teenagers will be able to leave too."

Hope smiled the best she could with her injuries. "Everyone will be free."

Astra wanted to tell her sister how bad it was on the

outside. She would know soon enough. Instead, she said, "It's not that great on the outside either."

Hope looked at her. "What about Ayden Webb?"

Jude shook his head. "We can't waste a minute on him. He's nothing without the guards or his followers."

"I have to go and sit with my group," Hope said.

Astra grasped her hand as gently as possible. After taking a seat at the end of the empty first row in the Prophecy bleacher on the left side of the room next to the door, one of the guards shut off the music.

Silence filled the space then the teenagers chanted over and over, "Holy is the Lord God Almighty! The wise Savior of Salvation will guide us! Holy, is the Lord God Almighty! The wise Savior of Salvation will guide us!"

The sense of evil trickled through Astra's veins. She couldn't wait to get away from this place.

Ayden Webb strolled down the long red carpet as if he was floating on water, his long robe flowing behind him like a train on a wedding dress. Dozens of candles were positioned on each side of the carpet. The flames flickering as he walked by. He headed up the stairs and sat on the throne. He was much older and taller than she had imagined; around fifty-five, slim, and a few inches taller than Jude.

The man raised a hand. The chanting stopped and everyone seemed to wait with bated breath for him to speak. After a few seconds, he lowered his hand. "You are the holy children of light, the chosen ones." His voice rose and fell as he spoke. "The sins of evil have been cleansed from the world with the second coming of Christ. You will rebuild the Earth, repopulate mankind. I will continue to guide you through the great transition."

Even the man's voice irritated her, the way sounded like he was an actor in a stage play, reciting his lines. Astra glanced at Jude and rolled her eyes. She could tell he could barely contain himself from laughing.

Ayden raised his hand again. "Brother Todd, under God's authority, let the food lottery begin." Todd stepped forward. "Holy children of light number sixteen and ninety-three."

Hope went to stand, and Astra stopped her. "You aren't fighting. This disgusting charade is ending."

The teenagers cried out, "Blessed be the Lord, who trains your hands for battle."

A frail girl in the Devine bleacher slowly stood. Panic etched her face. She made her way down through the bleacher and walked onto the stage. Cheering broke out.

When it quieted again, Astra stood and squared her shoulders. "Number 93 can't fight. She's injured."

Gasps surrounded her. Jude nudged her in the thigh to let her know he was going to light the fire.

Ayden Webb's pitless black eyes shifted to her and a strange darkness crossed his features.

Her heart thumped at the bone-chilling way the man was staring at her. A long beat of nervous silence passed.

Finally, he spoke, his tone eerily calm. "An unspiritual is among us from the outside."

Gasps erupted again from the bleachers. All eyes were on her. Astra had no idea what she was going to say. Her legs shook as she walked to the carpet in the center of the room and kept her hands clutched together. "Number 93 is injured. Perhaps the other two could fight first so she can prepare herself for the challenge." She lowered her head then looked up to continue. "God is watching. He would want you to share your guidance since you're the Savior of Salvation."

"God is watching everyone from an orbit close to Earth," Ayden Webb said.

The blood chilled in her veins. The more the man talked, the more unhinged he sounded. For good measure, Astra added, "Holy is the God Almighty."

His eyes locked on hers and it was as if he was staring right through her. All she could do was wait and hope.

A minute later, he pursed his lips and flitted his hand in the air. "Brother Todd, call the other two numbers. Under God's authority, let the food lottery begin."

Astra smirked under her mask. She doubted God or anyone else had given the man authority to treat anyone this way.

Todd took a few steps forward, stopped, and shouted, "Holy children of light number thirty-four and ninety-six.

The teenagers cried out again, "Blessed be the Lord, who trains your hands for battle."

This time, a girl and boy from each of the bleachers climbed down through the crowd. The boy was huge compared to the size of the girl; taller and wider. They slowly headed to the stage with apprehension in their step. The girl's eyes were wide with fright.

Astra returned to her seat and caught a faint whiff of smoke behind her. She turned her head and saw Hope's sweater on fire.

Jude snagged the corner of the flaming cloth and tossed it on top of the food boxes. The cardboard ignited instantly.

Worry stabbed Astra to the core. For a few horrifying seconds, she wondered if they could pull this off. A wave of sudden determination took over and she believed they could. They would.

As smoke rose and snaked through the bleacher, like fog, Astra gripped Hope's hand and her sister gave her a nod.

Someone yelled, "Fire!"

And all hell broke loose.

CHAPTER NINE

F ootsteps thundered as the bleachers emptied in front of Jude. Panicked teenagers ran, crying, and screaming to the side door desperate to escape. He shoved his hand into his pocket, seized the switchblade, and pulled it out. After thumbing the release, the knife clicked and sprung open. While flames leapt to life and consumed the food boxes, he kept his gaze steadfast at the end of the bleacher, waiting for Todd or any of the other guards to appear. Adrenaline and anticipation charged through his veins. Todd came into view, racing toward him.

"Help me put this out," Jude yelled. Intense smoke stung his eyes. He slapped his hand at the flames, stomped his feet at nothing, pretending he was trying to put out the fire. "One of the kids must have knocked over a candle."

"They probably did it on purpose." Todd stomped out some of the pieces of the boxes on fire. "God will forgive them for their sins. I won't. The little bastards."

Jude bolted into action. He lurched forward and looped his arm around the back of the man's neck, just under his chin. After ripping the mask off the man's face and tossing it on the floor, he pressed the knife blade against his cheek. "Drop the gun."

The rifle hit the floor with a bang.

"You will be punished for your sins. God sees everything," Todd said through gritted teeth.

Jude pushed the gun off to the side with his boot and squeezed his arm tighter around his neck, almost choking him. "Now, the key to the gate. Do it nice and slow."

Todd inched his hand into his right pocket then dropped the silver keyring at his feet. Out of the corner of his eye, Jude spotted Astra and Hope running to him.

Astra snatched the gun and keyring from the floor then raised the rifle and pointed the barrel at Todd's chest.

"The guards are blocking the door," Hope said, out of breath. "They told everyone the fire is under control and the food lottery is still going ahead,"

Jude shifted his gaze to the angry flames racing halfway up the wall a yard away.

Alarm shone in Astra's eyes. "I just saw one of the guards take Ayden Webb through a door behind the stage."

"Which guard?" Jude asked.

"The tall one." She gestured with the end of the rifle at Todd. "His pal."

He loosened his grip a bit on Todd's neck and the man sputtered, "Russell protects the Savior of Salvation. God ordered him to do so."

Jude grew tired of listening to him. "Knock it off with the religious crap. You're all bloody insane."

The smoke intensified, the oppressive heat becoming suffocating.

Hope coughed then pointed through an opening in the bleacher. "The carpet is on fire."

Jude noticed the one side of the stage was on fire too. "Hope, get his mask and turn it inside out. It'll give you some protection from the smoke."

Hope bent down and picked up the piece of cloth, looped it around her ears, and secured it over her mouth and nose.

"We have to get out of here. The whole place is going to go up," Jude said.

As Astra led the way, Hope followed.

Jude stayed behind them and kept a restrictive hold around Todd's neck, his muscles twitching and aching.

At the end of the bleacher, Astra stopped.

Jude stared, completely still. The young people were sitting on the floor, crying and coughing. Others had their heads bowed, praying. Spread out in front of the door, three guards blocked the exit with their guns pointed at the group.

Astra glanced over her shoulder.

Jude met her gaze and he hated what he was asking her to do especially after she had killed the man at the pharmacy. He couldn't let go of Todd. They already had two rogue guards and had no idea where Ayden Webb was now.

Astra's eyes searched his with a glint of recognition.

Jude gave her a nod.

A rapid repetition of gunshots exploded. One by one, the guards dropped to the floor. Screaming and shouting battled against the sound of crackling flames.

Astra lowered the rifle and screamed, "Get out of the building!"

* * *

In the tunnel, pounding footsteps caught up with them and a large group of teenagers coughing, with soot-covered skin and clothes, followed them into the parking lot. The last glimmers of daylight had transformed into early evening, fear and confusion electrifying the air. Dogs and cats ran around in the open space while some of the kids headed back to the camp for whatever reason. Fire shot out of one of the basement windows of the building next to the front door.

"Where's Todd?" Astra asked, her ears still ringing after shooting the guards.

Jude glanced at her. "I left him in the stairwell. He won't be a problem anymore."

At first, she was confused until she noticed the blood on his fingers. Astra didn't want to think about it, not now. She scanned the parking lot. "Where's Raider? We can't leave without him."

"I'll go and get him," Hope said. "He's probably playing with the other dogs."

Astra shook her head. "No way. I'm not letting you out of my sight. You stay with Jude, and I'll go. I'll be right back."

Jude grabbed her arm and stopped her. "You and Hope get the gate unlocked. Get as many as you can out. I'll find the dog."

Astra knew the last two guards could be anywhere and eventually they would catch up with them. She agreed even though she didn't want him to go. "Please be careful."

"I'll be back in a minute." He turned and sprinted toward the tunnel.

Waiting for Jude to return felt like hours. Astra paced and trembled a little, worried something had happened to him. Then she spotted him with Raider galloping beside him. Flames shot out of the building and lit the parking lot. Astra spotted a shadow, someone in a second-storey window.

A gunshot rang out.

Jude went down instantly.

The rifle slipped out of her hands and fell to the ground at her feet. She ran to him and dropped to her knees. Blood oozed from a bullet wound, just below his knee. "Oh, God, you're bleeding so much." Tears swamped her eyes, and she could barely see.

"My leg is broken. You have to go. I'll be okay. I'll figure it out." He dug into his sock and pulled out the keys to the truck. His hand shook as he handed them to her. "I promise I'll find my way home. Take Hope and go."

Astra took the keys, the thought of leaving him or him dying, almost paralyzed her. "Please don't make me do this. I love you, Jude Waverly. I can't leave you here."

He opened his mouth to say something, but nothing came out.

Another gunshot rang out coming from deep within the tunnel. Dogs scattered in every direction. The teenagers scurried out though the gate's opening.

Jude's eyes glossed over, and he gave her a pained smile as he clutched his leg with both hands. "I love you, Astra. I always have. You're my whole world. You mean everything to me. Save Hope. Now, go!"

Hope yanked on her arm. "Come on. They're coming. We have to leave."

Anguish wrenched Astra's heart. She felt her sister drag her to her feet. "I can get the truck and come back for you—I can shoot them."

"No. It's way too dangerous. There are still two guards plus Webb. We don't know where they are."

Panicked, Astra looked at her sister. "Go and get the rifle. I dropped it somewhere behind us."

Hope disappeared then reappeared a minute or two later. "The gun's gone. It's not there. Someone must have picked it up."

"Take my knife." Jude gritted his teeth and passed Hope the switchblade. "It's getting dark. It's not safe out there. Stay together no matter what."

Tears sprung in Hope's eyes, and she put the knife into the pocket of her track pants.

Another gunshot pierced the air, this time, the blast

too close.

Jude shoved hard at Astra's leg, pushing her away. "Run!"

Astra sucked in a ragged breath and felt as if she was suffocating. She grabbed Hope's hand and they bolted through the opening. Darting along the edge of the fence on the other side of the parking lot, she wiped the tears from her face. Once they were safe in the shadows of the building, Astra stopped. Her heart thudded in her chest. She placed both hands on the fence and watched.

Ayden Webb appeared with a guard on either side of him. They stood over Jude.

A gunshot blasted.

She turned away and the world fell apart around her, a tidal wave of grief knocking the air from her lungs. Then Astra, Hope, and Raider took off running as thick black smoke drifted high into the sky.

CHAPTER TEN

A week later...

At the back of the house next to the hidden entrance camouflaged from the rest of the world, Astra sat in a lawn chair with a rifle next to her and stared at the endless blue sky. Sunlight beamed down on her and warmed her bare arms. Flowers had bloomed, poking through the weeds in the gardens at the front and side of the house. Raider raced by chasing a squirrel determined to catch it.

Hope held up a fish in each hand. "Look what I caught us for lunch."

Astra raised a hand and shielded her eyes from the sun. Bulging eyes and bloated faces stared back at her. She wrinkled her nose and frowned.

"Sorry, I forgot you had a thing about food with faces."

Astra laughed. She'd finally given in and agreed to eat fish. Baby steps, she reminded herself. "It's okay. I'll get used to it. Just don't show me their faces next time, okay?"

"You got it. I'll get them ready for the oven." She licked her lips. "These bad boys are going to be delicious."

Astra smiled to herself and watched her disappear down the stair and into the bunker. The bruises around Hope's eye had faded, her lip was healed, and her swollen hands were back to normal. She was proud of her sister, the young woman she had become. They had spent hours every night, talking, catching up after five years of being apart. Hope's time in the camp still terrified her. It terrified Astra, too. They both understood it could take years for the horrible nightmares to go away, if they ever did.

The journey back to the bunker hadn't been an easy one. Her father's truck ran out of biodiesel, forcing them to walk over a mile until they had found another vehicle with more than enough fuel to get them home.

For the most part, Hope's mornings were spent down at the river, catching their meal for the day. They had wrangled two hens who had wandered onto the property, and Astra was grateful for an overabundance of fresh eggs. Hope had even built a small enclosure for the birds next to the garage.

Over the past three days, they'd been searching houses in the area and found some food, clothing, and other items they needed: shampoo, deodorant, toothpaste, medical supplies, a box of salt, and a huge bag of rice and flour.

It was still difficult to comprehend the true scale of the disaster even though they were living it. Astra wasn't sure they ever would. Life wasn't that bad, just different, tough, especially always wondering where their next meal would be coming from.

Winter would be the true test since Manitoba winters could be brutal. For now, summer was just around the corner, and Astra was looking forward to swimming in the river and going berry picking, the things she and Hope used to do together before the world flipped upside down.

Any doubt Astra had that she wasn't strong enough to survive in the new world had vanished back at The Closure and the pharmacy. She had been forced to grow up fast, become a different person, a person who would kill to protect the ones she loved.

A minute didn't go by when she didn't think about Jude. She loved him with all her heart and soul. They'd been together since grade school, spent five years, twenty-four hours a day together since the first day of the outbreak. She missed her best friend, missed hearing his voice, missed everything about him.

As each day passed, she continued to search for a spark of hope within her, the faith that had disappeared after her parents died. Astra refused to believe her time with Jude was over. She couldn't. More than anything she wanted to believe he was alive and one day he would come home. That was all Astra was seeking...the slightest sliver of hope.

THE END

AUTHOR NOTE

I hope have you enjoyed reading Seeking Hope. Be sure to leave a review!

Love reading post-apocalyptic dystopian novels? Don't forget to check out the thrilling Sum of all Tears Series (Icehaven and Liberty)! *"Fans of apocalyptic stories looking for a change from tales of melting ice caps will enjoy this cooler treat." (BookLife)*

Want to learn more about the author? Sign up for Kim's newsletter at www.kimcresswell.ca

OTHER BOOKS BY KIM CRESSWELL

The Whitney Steel Series
Reflection (Book One)
Retribution (Book Two)
Resurrect (Book Three)

The Raina Storm Series
Dawn of the Storm (Book One)
Dawn of the Enemy (Book Two)

The Assassin Chronicles Series
Deadly Shadow (Book One)

The Sum of all Tears Series
Icehaven (Book One)
Liberty (Book Two)

Single Title Novellas
Lethal Journey

The True Crime Quickie Short Story Series
Real Life Evil (Book One)

Murder on Sunset Strip (Book Two)
Garden of Bones (Book Three)
Edge of Madness (Book Four)
Chameleon (Book Five)
Backwoods Murder (Book Six)